MY HEART BEATS FOR AN ATLANTA BOSS

D. NIKA

K.C. Mills Presents
My Heart Beats for an Atlanta Boss
D.Nika

ACKNOWLEDGMENTS

THIS FEELS AMAZING.... MY 3RD BOOK!!!!!!

Let me first give all praises to the man above, without God none of this would be possible.

To my two babies Travon (Trae) and Trinity LaMya, I love y'all with everything I have in me and I do this for you both. Y'all make me proud every day and I hope mommy is making you guys just as proud.

To my AMAZING husband John, thank you, babe, for believing in me and pushing me to go for my dreams. You have been encouraging me for years to write a book and I thank you. I love you Zaddy. (I still ain't got that MacBook)

To my parents, thank you both for believing in me and pushing me to continue when I wanted to give up.

To my daddy Darrell Robinson... RIP daddy, I hope you

looking down from heaven smiling and proud of me. I miss you so much. Gone but never ever forgotten!!!!

To my bestie/sister Monique, you already know what it is. I love you babe

To my big cousins Lakesha and Tiffany.... What can I say, thank you for staying up with me all hours of the night, editing, letting me bounce ideas off of you, answering my many calls throughout the day, reading my work every single day. I know your email is full because of me. Thank y'all. I love you both to the moon and back.

A special thank you to Nikki Brown... you continue to help me whenever I ask. I am forever thankful to you.

Author Tina J man you drop knowledge on me daily and I hope to be where you are on them charts one day. Thank you for your kindness. Love ya babe!!!

K.C. Mills thank you for taking a chance on lil' ole me. I hope I make you proud Boss Lady, I'm tryna be like you when I grow up. LOL

To the readers thank you for giving me a chance. It gets better!!

Thank you to any and every body that has supported me, shared my post, and mentioned my book to somebody, etc. thank you thank you thank you.

Y'all know my mind be all over the place, so if I forgot anybody, just add your name here _____!!!!!!!!

I MADE IT!!!!!!!!!!!

SYNOPSIS

After surviving an abusive relationship, Nautica realizes she needs a fresh start where she can feel safe, taking a leap of faith she moves to Atlanta to be with her cousins, Amaris and Ahnais.

Ahnais is in a relationship with the love of her life Dravien, everything was going perfectly for them until Ahnais finds out that Dravien betrayed her in the worse way. Can Dravien prove that his intentions were not to hurt Ahnais? Is there something deeper behind his secret?

Amaris has dated a few guys here and there but not are the one. When Jaysun enters her life will he be able to prove that he is the one to change Amaris' life or will it be a failure like all the rest?

As Dravien's best friend Majik sees something special in Nautica and is ready to change her view of men but there's one problem standing in the way, CoCo, his worrisome baby mama.

Can Majik get CoCo out of the way and focus his love on Nautica? Will CoCo succeed at breaking up the new love before it even gets a chance to form? Will Nauticia's ex-boyfriend, Draego allow her to move on and finally be happy?

Nautica, Amaris, and Ahnais are all searching for love and dealing with all the drama that comes along with it. Then me in their lives all believe they can be what the girls need but at what cost? Can these three couples work things out or is their love just not meant to be? Come ride the love rollercoaster with these three couples in My Heart Beats for an Atlanta Boss.

PROLOGUE

 'm so fucking sick of being this motherfuckas punching bag every time he comes home drunk and pissed off about something. I have no idea what today's rant is about, I could hear him downstairs throwing shit around and cursing. I've been with this nigga since a month before my twentieth birthday, here I am twenty-six, and I'm still dealing with the devil.

Shit was never like this in the beginning of our relationship, and I can't tell you when shit went left. The first time Draego put his hands on me, I threatened to leave, but he promised to never do it again. That promise lasted for all of a year, and he was right back acting like Ike Turner.

I heard his ass coming up the stairs and braced myself for the bullshit I knew was coming. I sat at my vanity looking at the door through the mirror.

"Bitch, why the fuck don't I smell shit cooking in this got damn house?" Draego said pulling me by my hair and dragging me on the floor.

"Drae, please stop, I was about to start dinner. I just got home not too long ago!" I cried out.

I saw the look in his eyes, and I knew this was about to be a long ass night. I've gotten to the point where I don't know how to hide the mass number of bruises he constantly leaves on my body.

"Your stupid ass should have been home in time to do what the fuck you supposed to do. Now, what the fuck am I supposed to eat?"

"I can make you something really quick, just give-"

Before I could even get the sentence completely out, I felt the blow to my head. Repeatedly he punched me in my head and face like I was a man. I didn't even bother to beg him to stop, I knew that would just piss him off and make him go harder. I had just found out yesterday that I was pregnant and all I could think about was saving my baby. I didn't care about what he did to me, I just wanted to have my baby.

"Draego, please stop, I'm pregnant."

I prayed that me telling him he was about to become a father would somehow make him stop.

"You tryna trap me bitch, huh, did I tell you I wanted to have a baby with your muthafuckin hoe ass?"

The man that told me he loved me for six years was showing me everything but love right now. As he kicked me in my stomach over and over again, I tried to protect my unborn. Feeling blood running down my leg, I knew I failed miserably.

While Draego continued his assault on me, I didn't even try to block the blows anymore. The moment he killed my baby, I no longer cared if lived or died. I felt like everything thing inside me died with my baby. As I drifted in and out of consciousness, I welcomed death. Shit, anything was better than living and being with this unstable ass nigga.

Through my swollen eyes, I looked into the face of a hateful ass man as he hit me with the final blow that caused me to see nothing but darkness.

I woke up in the same spot, and I don't even know how long I have been laying here. I do know that Draego's punk ass didn't even have the decency to at least pick me up off the floor. That showed me that this nigga really didn't give a fuck about me. I've been talking to my cousin Amaris down in Atlanta, and she said I was welcome there anytime. If I don't leave now, this nigga would for sure kill my ass.

Pulling myself off the floor, I looked around for my phone. It was hard as fuck to see, considering I had a swollen eye. I had to muster up enough strength to get me some help. Looking all around, I saw my phone on the other side of the room and I crawled to it.

"911 how can I help you?"

"I-I need an ambulance"

"Ma'am what's the address where you need assistance?"

"422 Hazelwood Avenue"

I heard the operator asking more questions, but that is all I could give her. Before I knew it, I'd passed out again. When I woke up the second time, I was in the hospital, severely beat up, and no longer pregnant. The doctor informed me that they'd performed a D&C procedure and several other tests to make sure I was okay.

There was no fucking way I was going back to this bullshit. I grabbed my phone from the table next to my bed and made the call that I knew would change my life.

"Hey what's up cuz?"

"Hey Amaris, I'm ready. Is that offer still open, I need to get away and do it now?"

"Booking your flight now, go straight to the airport. I'll see you when you touch down."

That was all I needed to hear. I hung up quickly, jumped up and put on the clothes I came in with, bloody and all and got the fuck out of there. I hope I never saw this nigga again in my fucking life.

NAUTICA

*W*alking off that plane I felt more alive than I have felt in years. There was nothing like feeling safe. Leaving Chicago and more importantly, Draego, was the best decision I could have made. I know I deserve better than what I had been dealing with. Shit, I'm Nautica Renae Greene, I stand five feet six inches, medium brown skinned, college degree and a good head on my shoulders. I really don't need a man for shit. I will never again let a man bring me down.

I'm glad the paramedics had sense enough to grab my purse or I'd be fucked. I was able to grab a change of clothes and a few other items. I walked out of the baggage claim area with my shades on searching for my cousin Amaris. It's been so long since I've seen her, I couldn't wait to wrap my arms around her. We used to be super close until her and her sister Ahnais up and moved here to Atlanta. I spotted her, and when she saw me, she immediately ran toward me.

"Bitttttttchhh, bout time your ass stopped playing around and brought your ass here," Amaris said talking loud as hell. It don't matter where she at, this girl stays talking loud as shit.

"Girl, why your ass so damn loud. I told you I was coming, I'm glad I had the courage this time. That nigga would have killed me if I didn't leave but fuck that sad shit. It's time for me to get my shit together and turn the fuck up. Where Ahnais' ass at, she could have come with you."

"She with her so-called boyfriend Draiven, she acts like she can't do shit without his ass. I don't see how he make money being stuck up under her ass all fucking day." Amaris said sounding salty as hell.

I know she feeling some type of way since it's always been them two together.

I was ready to relax and see my family, especially my aunt, Frankie. She's my mama's baby sister, and when my mama died, she always looked out for me. I know she about to get in my ass when she sees my damn face. That's one lady that's always with the shits, it don't matter what's going on.

We made it to her truck and headed to her place. Looking around and taking in the scenery, I liked what I saw already.

"So cuz, are you here for a quick visit or are you here to stay and finally be done with that lame ass nigga?"

I thought I was gonna get away from having to answer questions about Draego's ass.

I went ahead and gave her the rundown on my entire relationship, I know I should have waited since I was going to probably have to tell this shit to my auntie again.

We blasted music all through the streets of Atlanta and cut up like we use to. It took no time to make it to my auntie's house. I wish we could have gone to Maris's crib first, so I could freshen up a little bit, shit pulling up it looked like they were having a full-blown party over here.

"Girl calm down, it's always jumping over here like this. Mama keeps a house full, niggas love coming over here to play cards and chill out. It's mostly Draiven's people." I guess she could see the uneasy look on my face.

"I'm good, I just don't want to be around a bunch of niggas looking like I ran away from the battered women's shelter,'" I told her as I looked around, beginning to become self-conscious about my looks.

"You fine cuzzo, we won't be here long, and shit you look better than half the broads these niggas fuck with."

I couldn't help but laugh as I saw some of the females clinging on to the niggas hanging outside. Just like Amaris said, some of these bitches were busted down, and they just knew they was looking good.

Walking in, I could see the niggas looking at me like they wanted to fuck me right there on the spot, while the hoes was looking at me with jealous eyes and hate. It amazes me that with a busted-up face and a slight limp from my bruised ribs, these females still hated.

I heard my Aunt Frankie's loud ass mouth, and I immediately

started smiling. I walked up behind her talking shit, just to get her ass going.

"Why you in here talking so damn loud old woman, they haven't put you in an old folks home yet?" I said trying to disguise my voice the best way I can.

"Who the fuck in my house talking shi-" she said turning around with cards in her hand and a cigarette dangling from her mouth.

"Only the prettiest niece you have ever had."

"Ahhhhhhh, is that my baby girl Nautica!"

She hugged me so damn tight I couldn't help but wince in fucking pain. By the look on her face, I could tell she noticed it right away. My auntie wasn't the type to bite her tongue, so I knew all hell was about to break loose. I was ready to go ahead and get this over with. I was tired of talking about the shit.

"What the hell is you wincing for, and why the hell you got on them binocular ass shades on? Take them shits off in my house."

I took them off and the look on her face, I would never forget. She didn't know what to say for once.

"Auntie, I-" I tried to explain, but she didn't want to hear shit from me.

"Shut the fuck up right now Nautica! Draiven, get the fuck in here nowwww!"

Hearing a bunch of feet shuffling through the house, I saw about five for six niggas come into the room. Ahnais came into the room behind them, and I was sort of glad for what I thought was going to be a good distraction.

"Nautica, when the fuck did you get here? Ain't nobody told me shit, and who the fuck did this shit to your face? Amaris you foul, why you didn't tell me this was why she was coming?"

"It wasn't my business to tell." She told Ahnais nonchalantly and sat down.

"All y'all shut the hell up, baby girl who did it? Tell auntie so I can get it handled."

It was like I lost my voice because I couldn't say nothing. I just looked around at all the eyes staring at me waiting for me to answer and I released the tears I had been holding since I left Chicago.

"Look shawty, you my girl's people, so that means you my people. We look out for ours out here, who did that shit to you?"

Who I learned to be Draiven said as we walked up to me with a hardcore look on his face, yet gentleness in his eyes. I could tell this nigga played no games, but he had a caring side to him, especially towards Ahnais.

"I might as well get this out, so I don't have to repeat the shit again. Look, my boyfriend, well now my ex-boyfriend Draego has been abusing me for a little over five years. Every time I tried to leave, he would find me. This time he left me for damn near dead, and I just want to move on with my life."

Once I got done spilling my business to my family and a bunch of strangers I didn't know, I looked up into the eyes of the finest man God could have created. He stared at me with his hazel eyes, rubbing the hairs of his goatee with the look of curiosity on his face.

There was no way I could continue looking at this man

considering how I was looking. I didn't come to Atlanta to look for another man anyway, having a relationship was the furthest thing on my mind.

"Go ahead and get you something to eat Nautica, we will leave this alone for now. Just know, if we ever see this so-called ex of yours I won't hesitate to have my son-in-law take care of his weak ass" auntie Frankie said, her ass just had to have the last word.

I did just what I was told to do cause my stomach was eating my back at the moment. Sitting down with my plate I took one last look at the mystery man and to my surprise, he was looking right back at me. Putting my head down to take a bite, I acted like I didn't see his ass. The last thing I needed right now was to be caught up with another man. He did look like he had some bomb ass dick though. I might just have to get the info on Mr. Fine ass and get a sample later on down the line.

MAJIK

A nigga was happy as fuck to be out here in these streets just chillin and not having to be worried about a muthafuckin thing. Too many muthafuckas out here didn't try me, but it was always that one bubble head ass nigga that wanted to prove some shit. Unfortunately for them, the only thing they proved was how quick it was to get their shit knocked back.

Shit, I'm got damn Majik Alexander, I'm that nigga out here in Atlanta. Didn't shit move out here unless it was either bought from me or I gave the okay for niggas to sell on my streets, and they still had to pay me a certain percentage to operate. I was a thirty-one-year-old, two hundred and fifty-pound nigga, standing six-feet-two with nothing but pure muscle.

Back in high school, a few lame ass niggas thought just because I was a light-skinned dude with pretty ass hazel eyes that

I was soft. After breaking a few jaws and a taking a few trips to the juvenile detention center, they stopped trying me.

I met Draiven's ass on one of my trips to juvie. He was my roommate, and I swear I couldn't stand that nigga when I first met him. We stayed getting into fights, and after I got jumped and he stepped in to have my back, we squashed our beef and been tight ever since.

I never had to worry about him crossing me and vice versa. Once we both got out of juvie, I convinced ma dukes to take him in, and he was like the brother I never had. It's always been me, him, and my cousin Lenyx running the streets together and getting into shit. The three of us started this drug shit together, and when one decides to get out, we all will get out.

I'm tryna see who shawty is that came in with Amaris and get some info on her ass. Looking in lil' mama's eyes, I can tell she been dealing with a lot. Even with all the bruises and shit on her, I can see her beauty. She must have been dealing with a lame ole sucka ass nigga, only a pussy nigga would do some shit like that. She don't give off the vibe that she is a ratchet ass female.

I sorta got a lil' situation myself going on right now, but soon that shit will be deaded. I been dealing with my ole' lady for about five years now and got a four-year-old lil'girl with her ass. I love my daughter, but I'm sick of her damn mama. I can't deal with that money hungry ass bitch no more. CoCo ass thinks 'cause I'mma boss out here that her ass can just sit up and spend my money. She got shit all fucked up. Her ass don't do shit but stay in them got damn stores and try to track my moves all day.

She knows today is my chill day and her pack hair wearing

ass thought she was about to roll up over here to Mama Frankie's with a nigga. She know they don't fuck with her like that. I done had to keep Maris and Ahnais from beating her ass a few times. She don't know when to shut the fuck up sometimes.

I done talked this aggravating ass girl up. A nigga can't breathe without her blowing up my got damn phone. I let her simple ass call me about four times back to back before I decided to answer the phone.

"Yo, why the fuck are you calling me back to back like yo' stupid ass really want something CoCo?" I answered not even giving her a chance to say anything.

"Well if you would have answered the first time, I wouldn't be calling your ugly ass back to back. You must be around some funky ass hoes that got you not wanting to answer."

"Nah, I'm not around no hoes at the moment, but that could change at any given second. I am looking at one fine ass woman across the room right about now though." I said while taking another look at shawty.

"Why the fuck are you so disrespectful?"

"Why the fuck are you so annoying? What the fuck you call me for CoCo, matter of fact where the fuck is my baby at?"

I know her ass was either calling to see if I'm with a bitch or calling me for some money. I wasn't the type of nigga that didn't take care of his woman, don't get me wrong, I use to be so in love with this woman. I just knew she was going to be my wife one day. Shit, that love went away just like her drive for wanting to do something with her damn life. The more money I made, the more she became useless and needy.

"Majesti is with your mother, she wanted to take her to some function they were having for kids at her church. Can you transfer me some more money in my account, I wanted to go shopping with my girls?"

"Nope, what else can I help you with?"

I meant what I said, I was through being her damn ATM. She better start putting money in the account instead of always taking it out.

I listened to her beg for a few more minutes before I got tired of the conversation.

"Look Co, you saying the same thing over and over and the answer hasn't changed and it ain't gonna change. I'm for real through with this got damn conversation with your ass."

"Don't say shit when I go out and find me another nigga."

I guess this bitch thought her threat was supposed to move me. I still wasn't giving her ass shit.

"Shit, please hurry up and do the shit. You want me to help you find that nigga? Get the fuck off my line and have my got damn daughter home by the time I get there!"

I hung up the phone 'cause I was done with the back and forth. I already gave her ass too much of my time. Her ass wanted me to sit up and argue with her, but I wasn't beat for that bullshit.

I went back to play a few hands of spades before I left to check the streets. I needed to make sure shit was straight before I go spend time with my baby girl. I made it a point to give her quality time every chance I get. She wasn't going to grow up looking for love from a no good ass nigga 'cause she got daddy issues fuck that. Majesti is my heart.

I noticed every time somebody got close to lil'shawty, her ass would jump and shit. Whoever her ex-nigga was really fucked up her mental. I made a note to get with the homies to find out about her lil'fine ass.

AMARIS

J'm glad my cousin finally brought her ass to Atlanta with us. Shit is about to get real lit down here. Me, my sister Ahnias, and Nautica use to be real close before we moved. We still talked all the time though.

Once she healed from all of her bruises, we definitely gotta show bitches how the Jones girls get down.

We were always the outcast of our family because our cousins figured because we three were pretty as hell, they thought we acted stuck up. Which was far from the truth. We occasionally talked to the others from time to time.

I was just a normal light-skinned girl, about five feet and four inches of nothing but pure beauty. I had a small oval face and pretty curly long hair. I can't tell you what I was mixed with because we never knew our punk ass daddy. I had a small figure, but enough ass to keep a nigga satisfied.

I peeped how Majik was eyeing her down, and I wonder if she saw it too. I know his ass wasn't tryna holla at my fam, cuz I know for a fact he got an ignorant ass baby mama. I've been trying to beat her ass for a while now, so it's best he keeps it moving.

I'm ready for this shit to be over with. I got yet another got damn date tonight. I already know it's going to be something about this nigga I don't like. I met his ass at this lil' coffee shop downtown on my way to work one morning. I was already running late and really wasn't in the mood to talk to anybody, but he was so persistent I just had to give him my number.

After my last boyfriend Terrance decided he wanted to have me and a wife, without informing me I was a sister wife, I've been real cautious about who I deal with. You damn near have to give me your social security number before I even give you my phone number.

This muthafuckas' wife knocked on my door with their three chaps talking about I was ruining her family. I was trying to be nice to the bitch at first and inform her dumb ass that I didn't know his ass was married. Unfortunately for her, she wanted to talk shit and swing on me. That got her a well-whipped ass whooping.

"Why yo' ass sitting over here looking crazy? You always somewhere looking like you mad at the damn world." Lynx said walking up with the bullshit.

We used to fuck around for a lil' bit when Ahnias first met Majik. Shit didn't last long cause like the rest of these niggas out here in these streets, his ass didn't wanna do right. We continued fucking around, but I had to cut that shit off.

I heard he got a lil' girlfriend now name Tori. Now ain't that some shit? His ass didn't wanna do right for me, but now this nigga wanna be Mr. Faithful. I was mad about the shit for a lil' bit, and sometimes I like to make him think I'm still hot about it, just to fuck with his mental. I had to let the shit go though and realize, what's for me is for me. The shit just wasn't meant to fucking be.

"Why the fuck you over here talking to me? Where your lil'-girlfriend Tori at?"

I just couldn't resist fucking with him. His cat-eyed ass knows he fine as fuck though.

"Mannn here you go with that bullshit."

"Whatever, what you want Lenyx?"

"I ain't want shit for real, just checking on yo' ass."

We sat and talked for a lil' bit until he got a call from his lil' girlfriend.

After kicking it with the family for a few more hours, Nautica and I left so I could get her settled and get ready for this damn date. I had it in my mind to stand this nigga up, but he done texted me a few times making sure I was really gonna show up.

I got in the shower and washed with one of my Bath and Body Works shower gels. Lord knows I loved me some damn Bath and Body Works. I spent about twenty damn minutes getting my hygiene together. I didn't know what the hell I wanted to wear. I didn't wanna be too sexy and give this nigga the wrong idea.

"Nauti, come here for a minute."

I wanted to get her opinion on a few of my outfit choices. This girl loved her some damn fashion. I know she was about to get me all the way together. I hope I could convince her ass to maybe go to school and get her degree in fashion.

"I damn near dozed off trying to get all my shit put up. I didn't even bring all my things and still got a lot. What's up though?"

"I need your help, which outfit you think I should wear?"

"Ewww, neither one of these. Move out the way, I got this." She said rushing all the way in my room. Her ass was a little too damn excited.

After she got me all the way together and touched up my hair, I put my jewelry on, grabbed my phone and left out to meet Jaysun.

I never let a guy I'm just meeting pick me up for a date. I never know how the date may go and needed to be able to leave when I wanted to, and if I didn't like his ass, I didn't need him knowing where the hell I lived at.

I made it to the restaurant in no time, his ass was going all out 'cause this shit looked fancy as hell. He may get a few points from me off the top. I sent him a text and let him know that I have arrived and was told to come in. He was actually already there, that was rare for niggas to actually be on time or early.

Meeting me at the door with roses, he kissed me on the cheek and led me to our table. I looked at this man for real for the first time, and this muthafucka was some kinda fine. Like take his ass home on the first fucking night and ride his face fine.

"Well hello, Ms. Amaris. I'm glad you finally took me up on my offer for a date. How'd I get so lucky?" he asked and gave me a deep dimple smile, and I be got damn if this nigga didn't have some white perfect ass teeth.

It ain't nothing like a fine ass nigga with some perfect white teeth. I'm bout to ask this man to give me his babies.

"I guess it was just your lucky day. I can't be just giving my time to someone who don't deserve it you know." I gave him the smile that takes niggas down to their knees.

"Well I'm glad I got the chance beautiful. So, tell me a little about yourself if you don't mind."

"There's not much to tell, I'm twenty-five and a registered nurse. I have one sister and a niece who I love with my all. I was raised by a strong single woman. I have a love for animals and art."

I sat there for about five more minutes talking about animals and realized I had been talking nonstop. It was something about my love for animals and art that had me always talking nonstop once I started.

"I'm sorry, I've just been talking my head off. Tell me a little about yourself and come with the truth. I know how y'all men can be."

"Ahh, here you go. I'm thirty-one and let's just say I'm in pharmaceuticals. I'm a single father of a beautiful eight-year-old little girl. I love everything music. I'm thinking about investing in a music studio and starting a record label. It's a lot of talent here in Atlanta, and I want to be the one to tap into that."

"What happened to her mother if you don't mind me asking?"

"Her mom passed during childbirth. It's been hard raising her without her mother, but thankfully my mom is alive and helps me out a lot. My baby girl has had it rough this past year. We found out she has leukemia. The doctor visits and treatments take a toll on her."

He went on to tell me more about his baby girl, and my heart literally broke for him. I could not imagine having to deal with that with my niece Ayanni or my own for that matter. Learning more about him made me drop my guard just a little bit, I was more into the date than I was when I first got here.

After we got the introductions out the way, we turned the conversation to a lighter note. Although we were still getting to know each other better, it didn't seem like a first date. We laughed and joked the whole time. Before I knew it, we had been here for three hours. I had missed five calls from my mama and three from Ahnais.

I already know it's about to be some shit with them. I hate being the baby 'cause they make sure they treat me like one.

"I'm sorry, can you excuse me for a second. My mom and sister have called me several times, and if I don't call one of them back, they will definitely be up here."

"No problem gorgeous, take your time."

I stepped away to the bathroom and called my mama back and of course as soon as she answered she cursed me all the way out. Once I told her I was on a date and actually enjoying it, she let up a little and let me off the phone. She made me promise to call her as soon as I got home, and her rude ass hung up in my face.

Once I made it back to the table, I noticed Jaysun was on a call. I tried to get back up and give him his privacy, but he waved me back down.

"Okay baby, try to lay down with nana and get you some sleep. Nana will give you something for your pain and daddy will be home in a little while. Yes, baby, you can lay in daddy's bed. I'll see you in a few. Yes, I promise Destiny. Daddy loves you. See you later."

He ended his call and directed his attention back to me.

"I'm sorry about that, my daughter isn't feeling too well."

"No, I understand. It is getting pretty late. I should be getting out of here anyway."

"Well I certainly enjoyed myself, I hope we can do this again soon." He said while paying the check.

"Well, I guess since you are pretty charming and you're not too bad on the eyes, I think I can give you that." We both laughed and headed for our cars.

"Goodnight beautiful, please text me and let me know you made it home safely." He said and kissed me on the cheek.

Once I unlocked my door, he made sure to open it for me being the perfect gentleman. Even though I know this man had a lot of street in him, he was also a true gentleman.

I drove home with a huge ass smile on my face. This is the first time in a while that I enjoyed myself with the opposite sex.

Once I made it home, I made sure I called my mama's crazy ass to let her know I was back. I told her about my date, hung up with her and got ready for bed.

Lying in bed, I sent Jaysun a text message letting him know I made it in and to have a good night. I made sure to also ask him was his daughter okay. We texted back and forth, until I fell asleep smiling.

AHNAIS

$\mathcal{I}$ swear this nigga Draiven about to make me fuck his ass up. Today was supposed to be his chill day with me. He thinks he fucking slick, talking about he needed to go check on some shit in the streets. His stupid ass don't even know I that I know his ass cheating. I been with this nigga for damn near four years and I thought shit was good.

He got to be a stupid ass nigga to cheat on a bitch like me. I'm an educated woman with my own shit. I've been a pharmacist for the last six years, with another degree in business. Not only was I smart, I know I was bad as hell. Shit, I ain't conceded, I just know what it is. I'm light-skin with that good long hair bitches get on their knees and pray for. I stand five-seven with a banging ass body. Any nigga would be happy to have my ass and here he is fucking up.

I've called this nigga about five times, and he keeps sending me to voicemail. It's okay though, I got a trick for his ass.

I spent the last two hours politely packing up his shit. I damn near had half of his shit done when I heard his ass come in the house. I didn't bother to stop when he came in the room, fuck him, shit.

"Ayee man what the fuck you doing with my shit Nias?" he asked walking up on me.

I continued to ignore him just like he'd been doing me for hours.

"Man, I know you hear me talking to you. What the fuck is your problem?"

"Shit it's obvious you don't wanna be here or in this relation-ship anymore, so I'm just helping you out by packing up your shit!" I yelled out.

"Girl, what the fuck is you talking bout? If I didn't wanna be here, I wouldn't be."

He walked up on me and snatched his clothes out my hand. I love this man so much that my emotions came out and I didn't want them to. I didn't want to show him how much of a hold he really had on me. It would be hard to be without him, but as much as I love him, I love myself more.

Before I knew I had a rush of tears rolling down my face, I damn sho' tried to hurry up and wipe my face before he saw me crying.

"Yo, what the fuck is you crying for?" he asked wrapping his arms around me.

"Where have you been Drae? More importantly, what was so important that you couldn't answer my calls?"

"I told you I had to handle some shit, why you buggin' about that?"

"I'm not the beat around the bush type of bitch, so I'mma just put it out there. I know you cheating on me Draiven, and before you try and lie, I already saw the messages on your phone."

"What messages Ahnais? Ain't nobody cheating on you!"

If he wanted to play these games, he could play them by himself. I was not the one for the bullshit.

"Okay Draiven, you can play dumb all you want to, but know this, when you look up one day, and I'm gone, just remember it was because of you.

He continued trying to talk to me, and I ignored the fuck out of him. He wanted to pull disappearing acts, well I'm bout to show him how the shit feels. I put together a bag without him even knowing and left the house.

As I got in my car and pulled slowly away from the curb, I started reflecting on my life. Even though I know for a fact I didn't need Draiven financially, I know it'd hurt me to leave him. He is so good with my daughter Ayanni. All she ever wanted was somebody to call daddy.

She never had a father due to the fact that she was conceived through rape. It took me a long ass time to get over that shit, but I eventually did.

I had been studying for a final all night on campus and didn't leave until well after two in the morning. I was feeling good about the amount of studying I'd gotten done that I wasn't at all paying attention to my surroundings. Unfortunately for me, that got me pulled behind a building and raped and beat up. I opened my eyes enough to see my attacker, and I would remember his face anywhere. He was never caught, and it took me years before I could even be out by myself without looking over my shoulders or making sure I stayed around a bunch of people.

When I got with Draiven, Ayanni took to him right away and was calling him daddy within the first year. Even though I know it will hurt her, I have to think of me first. I be damn if I let him play my ass for a fool.

I made it to my mama's house to talk to her for a while, and I noticed Amaris' car parked in the driveway. I'm glad her ass was here because I need to hear about this lil' date her ass went out on.

Walking in the house Ayanni noticed me first, I love when my baby girl is happy to see me. That let me know I am doing something right.

"Mommy, mommy, I've been waiting for you all day. May I ask what took you so long?" she asked putting her hands on her hips, with her head tilted to the side like she was grown.

"Well little girl, I was busy with daddy if you must know," I said picking her up and kissing her pretty lil' face.

"And where is daddy? I called him, and he didn't answer, he promised that he'd call me today and come see me."

The pout on her face when she mentioned her daddy not

calling is the reason I hate Draiven has put us in this situation. She's mad about a phone call, imagine what it will be like if she couldn't see him every day.

I sat and talked to my baby girl about her night with her Glam-ma for about ten minutes before I went to find my mama and sister. I needed some sister time, and I needed it like yesterday. I was scared as fuck to tell my mama about what happened between him and me because that lady was crazy as hell. She's the type that would cut his ass on sight.

"What y'all in here talking about?" I asked them walking into the room.

"I was just about to tell them what I did the other day when I was late for work," Amaris said laughing so hard she couldn't even start the story.

"I wish you would shut the hell up with all that damn laughing and tell the fucking story. You sound like a wounded fucking hyena!"

Mama was getting irritated, I'd only been in the room for a few minutes and hell even I was getting annoyed. Shit, I damn near didn't wanna hear the shit now.

"Okay, okay. So last week I was late for work and couldn't afford another point or write-up, so I called my boss and told him that I had a death in the family. He sent his condolences and said I just needed to bring proof. I was just going to go print off an obituary right," at this point she started laughing so hard, and I couldn't help but laugh too, just because I already knew her ass had done some crazy shit. "So, I saw in the paper somebody had died with our last name. Tell me why I went to this lady's funeral who I didn't know and got the obituary to take back to work."

"Amaris, I hope you didn't do no fucked up shit like that? Bitch, you going straight to fucking hell." I was laughing so hard; my ass had tears in my eyes.

"I sure did hoe, I had to make sure I paid my respects to my dear ole aunt, Bernice Jones. I sat my ass right there in the back with my Gucci shades on, looking on Instagram. When I went back to work, my punk ass boss gone ask me how my aunt passed. I said dear ole aunt Bernie died of natural causes. It's a good thing it was said at the funeral a few times. My ass wasn't about to lose my damn job, fuck that."

I was for real done with this hoe. You gotta be a crazy kinda of muthafucka to go to a stranger's funeral.

We sat back and talked to Nautica about her future plans and that somewhat took my mind off of my own problems, at least for the moment. I was glad that my cousin's body had finally healed because I was in need for a night out.

"So, are you hoes up for a night out? I need to get out and have a couple of drinks."

"Here she goes with this bullshit," mama said lighting up a cigarette, I wish she'd let that habit go. "What the hell is wrong with you? You been looking stupid in the damn face since you brought your crinkled haired ass up in here."

"Mama, do it really take all that to just ask me what is wrong?"

"Hoe don't come up in here telling me how to talk. Now like I said what the fuck wrong with your ass?"

I looked around to make sure Ayanni wasn't anywhere being nosey. I would never taint her image of her father, I wasn't that type of bitch.

When I noticed she was nowhere in sight, I went ahead and told them what was going on.

"Well to cut a long story short, Draiven been acting funny lately, so I decided to check his phone. Come to find out his ass been out here cheating. I don't know with who, all I know is that he is doing it. He, of course, denying it. I confronted him, he lied about it, and I left. End of the story. Now where y'all wanna go?"

Before I could even finish what was saying, my crazy ass mama had done pulled out her gun from under the couch. I don't know why her old ass thought she was a gangster. Looking at her putting her hair into a ponytail, all I could do was laugh. This lady was for real was loco.

"Why the hell is your ass still sitting down?

"Mama, really? What are you about to do?" I don't know why Amaris even asked her that, she knows just like I do how Frankie is.

"Are you okay Ahnais?" Nautica had nothing but concern in her eyes when she asked that question. With all that she is going through, I don't want to burden her with my problems.

"I'm fine y'all, if we work through it cool, if not, I'm ok with that too. I'm not gonna dwell on the shit. I'm gonna show his ass what it feels like to be without me for a while though. Maybe that will make him get his shit all the way together."

"I like my plan better, I told his wobble head ass when you

brought him here not to fuck up, or I was gonna shoot his ass. He must have thought I was a joke, so Ima show his ass!"

I let my mama keep rambling on while I ignored her ass, the truth is, she is going to do what she wanted anyway.

We planned our night out, and then I went to spend time with my baby girl. She loved being at home, but she loved being over here with her Glam-ma more. That's because my mama let her ass do whatever hell she wanted to do. That's why her ass so damn grown now. Between Frankie and Amaris, I don't know who is worse.

After three damn board games, playing spa, and watching a few movies, my ass was officially exhausted. I knew I was gonna need a power nap in order to turn up like I wanted to tonight.

I got my ass in bed, turned my phone on vibrate, and took my ass to sleep.

DRAIVEN

I don't know how the fuck my stupid ass got in this fucking situation. Well shit, I do know, I let my dick get me fucked up. The whole time I've been with Ahnais, I ain't ever thought about fucking another bitch.

This bitch Tatiana that bag up our dope at one of our warehouses been on my dick for about a year. I flirted with the bitch a few times, but that was about it. She would show me that pussy every chance she got, being as though we made them bitches work naked, that wasn't a hard task for her to do.

I ignored her advances every time she tried to fuck a nigga, and for the life of me, I have no idea how the fuck I slipped up. I swear I think the bitch drugged my ass. I can't remember shit from that night.

This bitch got all kind of pictures and videos of me doing some fucked up ass shit, ain't no way in hell I can let this shit get back to my damn girl. The thot ass bitch calls herself tryna black-mail a nigga. One minute the bitch sending messages tryna get me to come fuck with her ass and the next her ass tryna get shit out of a nigga.

I gotta tread lightly with this shit though cause this bitch know way to fucking much about our shit, her ass will never live to tell about it, but that's beside the fucking point. T

Ahnais' crazy ass has been gone for about a month. She got me fucked up though. This shit ain't never gonna be over. I still get to spend time with my baby girl, but that shit ain't the same. They need to have their asses home, and as soon as I get done with this fuck ass meeting, that is exactly what the fuck is about to happen.

After I jumped in the shower and washed my ass, I grabbed a lil' fit for the day. I wasn't tryna do too much, so I put on a Nike jumpsuit and threw on my Jordan elevens. I sprayed on a lil' bit of that Guilty Gucci cause a nigga had to stay smelling good. I hated wearing a lot of jewelry, so I only rocked my Rolex watch. After grabbing my wallet and my keys, I set my alarm and headed out.

I didn't know which car I wanted to ride in today, so instead of trying to decide, I jumped on my Suzuki Hayabusa. I loved the hell out of this motorcycle. I got it custom made, and a few months after I got it, I went and got my baby girl a miniature one just like mine.

Speeding through the streets of Atlanta, I had the song *Rock by Plies* blasting through my speakers. As I really listen to the words, this shit described my shawty to the T. It wasn't too many niggas that could listen to music on their bikes. My shit was bad.

Pulling up to the warehouse, I made it there in no damn time. I had so much shit on my mind I really didn't even know how I made it here in one fucking piece.

Stepping into the building, I saw everybody who worked for us in attendance, even that sloth looking ass bitch Tatiana. Bitch smiling at me and shit like we friends, least she could do was fix her got damn teeth before she started smiling tryna be sexy and shit. I didn't notice her fucked up grill when I was flirting with her ass.

Pulling up a chair next to the boys, I was more than ready to get this shit over and done with. I didn't give a shit about nothing going on in this muthafuckin room.

"So, some shit was brought to my attention, and I gotta say it didn't make a nigga too happy to hear." Majik started to say as he pulled out those got damn gold plated Baoding balls.

If this nigga had those fuckin stress balls in his hand that meant his ass was pissed the fuck off about something, and somebody was about to fuckin die.

"Brother, what do I always say I hate the most in life?" looking at me, he was waiting for me to answer. He knew I wasn't the one for this mind game bullshit.

"Snitches, thieves, and snakes bro. Snitches, thieves and snakes." Lighting up my blunt I sat back to see where this shit was going. I'd know if I would have been answering my phone, but the last couple days I'd been running up behind Ahnais' ass.

"It seems we have a few snakes amongst the team. I feed all

you muthafuckas well, and you wanna cross me!" this nigga had for real spit coming up out of his damn mouth.

Yo, I got a for real phobia of niggas spitting on me. Man, a while back I was choppin it up with this saliva mouth ass muthafucka, and I swear that fool ass nigga spit on my got damn lip. My ass ain't been right ever since. I stand three feet away from people when they talking to me.

This nigga was on the other side of the table, and I still scooted my damn chair back a little. Lenyx looked at me, laughed, and shook his head. He knew how I felt about that bullshit.

Majix was still yelling and preaching about loyalty getting closer and closer to me. I promise you if this nigga spit on me, he gonna have to dig a bullet out his ass cause I'm shooting his ass today.

I looked over at Thotiana, and her ass was looking nervous as fuck. That shit piqued my interest. I was definitely bout to look into her ass. If her ass on some funny shit with the team, I'm killing her ass. Well shit, I'm killing her ass anyway, so she outta fucking luck.

I was in my thoughts when I heard shots fired.

PHEW PHEW PHEW

Looking up, I saw that nigga Taz on the floor leaking with bullet holes in his chest and one in his head.

I peeped over at Lenyx ass, so he could give me a hint on what's going on, this nigga just shrugged his shoulders and started eating his chips. Shit, I guess I'd have to wait until this meeting to find out what the fuck is really going on.

To kill time, I sent my shawty a text to see what she was on.

Me: I'mma pick up you and Yanni to grab a bite to eat if that's cool wit you.

My Wife: You can pick up Yanni

Me: When you gonna get off this bullshit man, I ain't een do shit.

My Wife: When you ready to tell the truth then we can talk.

Me: I'll be by there tonight man

I needed to hurry up and dead this situation. This exactly why a nigga don't cheat, I don't have the patience for the shit.

LENYX

The shit cuz laid on me had my damn heading spinning. Muthafuckas was coming after us out of nowhere. We had niggas try us from time to time, but we were always able to nip that shit in the bud before it got too far. We got niggas gunning for our head, and we ain't got a clue where the shit coming from.

Regardless of who the fuck it was, their mamas better have that black dress ironed and ready to wear. In the midst of us tryna figure out who the snakes were, we ended up finding out that lil' nigga Taz been stealing from us. How the hell he gonna bite the hand that feeds him. This dude came to us about two years ago crying and begging for a job. I even threw his ass a few extra bands from time to time to help him pay for his mama's medical bills.

His bitch ass is lucky I didn't get to him first. Folks think

Majik is crazy, shit our dads are twin brothers. We look so much a fuckin like that people often mistake us for brothers. That nigga is the quiet type crazy, but me, I'm that I don't give a fuck type crazy.

I was raised by a single father after my hoe ass mama ran off with another nigga. The bitch had the nerve to try to come and form a relationship with me a few years ago after the nigga left her. She came out the gate with her hands out, what the fuck she was expecting.

I sent that hoe right on her way. My pops did damn good raising me, I didn't need her ass. That nigga was there for all my firsts. My first scrape, heartbreak, night behind bars, he was there. When I walked across that stage to get my high school diploma, he was right there in the first row. The nigga got there three hours early just to be in the front. When I tell you I didn't need her ass, I don't need her for shit.

People say I act and look just like his ass. Hell, that wasn't a bad thing at all 'cause I was one fine ass nigga. Shit, I walked my six feet one, two-hundred-pound, light skin, hazel-grey eyed ass out my house every muthafuckin day like I'm the shit.

My ass could have been anything I wanted to be, hell I had the highest GPA in not only my school, but the district. They wanted me to be the valedictorian, but I declined that shit. Ain't no way in hell I was about to get up in front of a bunch of mutha-fuckas who I knew for a fact didn't give a shit about me. It was plenty of times that them whack ass teachers accused me of cheating because my damn grades were so fucking high, or I heard they ass whispering about me not being shit but a little ghetto boy with luck.

I even made sure I went to college to get a degree in business, not because it was something I really wanted to do, but because I know I needed to have a backup plan. I ain't planning on staying in this shit forever.

Once shit got situated with these fuck ass workers, I needed to holla at my lil' shawty, so I headed to the crib to get this shit over with. I been with Torrie for a little over a year and shit already going downhill. At first, her ass made it seem like shit was all about me, but as the time goes by, I'm starting to see different.

Every time I turn around, her ass asking for something. When I met her, she was in school trying to get her degree in Cosmetology. Now all she does is take her ass down to the mall and clubbing with CoCo's thot ass.

Since her and CoCo are cousins, I should have known better, but she went out her way to show me that she different. A lie don't care who fucking tell it.

I was about two blocks away from the house, and she started blowing my shit up.

"What is it, Torrie?" I answered with an attitude. I told her ass I was on the way so her calling me was unnecessary.

"Did you really have to answer the phone like that Len? Where are you?"

I never realized until now how annoying this bitch was.

"What the fuck did I tell you I was doing? Didn't I say I'd be there in a few? Stop calling me asking dumb ass questions, man!" Hanging up the damn phone, I was not about continue that conversation with her ass.

Pulling into my driveway, I turned the car off and finished off a blunt I had earlier. I was in no rush to go inside, so I sat back and admired my big ass house. Before Torrie brought her needy ass to my shit, it was just me in that big ass house. I wanted this to be the spot I raised a family in, and I thought she would be the one.

Since I saw her peeking out the blinds, I went ahead and got out to head inside. I can't stand for somebody to interrupt my peaceful time.

I knew she was in the family room waiting on me, so I went to the kitchen and got me something to drink just to be an asshole. I drunk that shit as slow as I could. Finally finishing the shit, I took my ass in there to get this shit over with.

"What the fuck is it that you need to discuss so fucking bad man?"

"First of all, all that ain't even necessary. I need to talk to you about us, shit don't seem the same no more Lenyx."

Here she go with this bullshit. I hate when bitches ask dumb ass questions they already know the fucking answer to. I kept looking at her like she was stupid, not even offering up a damn response.

"So why the hell you sitting there looking at me like you don't hear me talking to you?"

"Cause the shit you saying, I really ain't tryna hear. Yo, on some real shit man, what is this shit about, I got shit to do?

Sitting here talking about dumb shit ain't on my list, so get to the point of this Dr. Phil ass talk."

I had to light up another blunt in order to deal with this conversation. This shit was already giving me a headache, and it just started less than five minutes ago.

"We've been together for a while, and you said you loved me, I'm just curious to know why don't I have access to your bank account or any of our money for that matter." She said with a frown on her face and her arms crossed.

I choked on my weed I started laughing so damn hard. Was this trick ass bitch serious? If I didn't know before, I damn sho' know now what her ass was really the fuck on.

I had to wait until I got my coughing under control before I could fully respond to her. Wiping away the tears I had in my eyes from laughing so hard, I was finally ready to give her a response.

"I'm confused, when did you put any money into that account? When did you get your ass up and go to work, as a matter of fact, when the fuck are you gonna get a job?" I sat on the edge of the couch and put the elbows on my knees because I was for real waiting on this damn answer.

"Why should I work when I have a nigga that can and do take care of me?"

See this is why I should have stayed my ass single. I don't mind taking care of my woman, but I wasn't about to take care of a selfish, lazy, self-entitled ass female who thinks the world owes them something.

"See this is where you got shit fucked up, I suggest you start filling out some job applications and start looking for your next meal ticket shawty cause I'm not that nigga. You got three days to have you and your shit out my house!"

I wasn't about to argue with this dense ass broad neither was I about to try to explain to her where she fucked up at. It was no point, she'd never get it anyway.

"You think you can just kick me out and dump me like that nigga? If you do, then you got shit all the way fucked up. Remember I know what it is that you really do, fuck around and have the Feds at your door before the sunset."

She crossed her legs with a smug look on her face like she just won the lottery. The only thing she just won though, was a free ride to hell. Her stupid ass just signed her own death certificate. I knew I couldn't do the shit right now though if I did, I'd be behind them bars. I had to plan this shit out, I didn't know how I was gonna do it, but what I did know what this bitch was gonna be eating them lil' slimy ass bugs for dinner soon.

I stood up, and I could see the look of uncertainty on her face. Yeah, that's right bitch, be afraid, be very fucking afraid. I smiled kissed her on the cheek and looked at her in the eyes.

"You're right baby, I'm tripping, I'm sorry. Let's pause this conversation for another day, but just know I heard you. I'll get you added to the account sometime this week."

"Thank you, baby, that's all I ask." She said squealing, jumping up and down.

I had a few things I needed to handle today, but it looks like I gotta put that shit on pause. I need to handle this shit and handle it quick. I was not about to let no one jeopardize the freedom of me and my brothers. We worked too hard to become some boss ass niggas.

I sent a group text out to them niggas letting them know we had a problem.

Me: Man I gotta get an exterminator ASAP. Got a bad case of rodents in my crib.

Majik: Get up wit me later. I need to know how bad it is to determine who we need to call.

Draiven: can't stand damn rodents. Mufuckas stink man. You gotta get rid of them shits quick bro!!

Me: shit gonna be hard to get rid of

I put my phone up and started thinking of a few ways to make this shit easy. Being that she's CoCo's fam, this shit put us in a difficult spot. Until I get this shit handled though, I needed mufuckas to see us happy and together. I could put up a front for a few days.

"Ayee T, you wanna go grab a bite to eat?"

This hoe jumped up ready to go spend somebody else's money. It's all good though, her ass better make the best of her last meal, cause her ass about to be nothing but a memory.

NAUTICA

I've enjoyed myself here since I been in Atlanta, makes me mad that I didn't make this move sooner. Getting settled here wasn't as hard as I thought I would be. It didn't take me no time to get a job thanks to Amaris. She ended up getting me a job at the hospital where she works.

I wasn't a registered nurse like her but registering these sick ass folks in was good enough for me. I was thinking about going back to school, I just didn't know what the hell I wanted to do. I didn't want to waste my time just doing anything though.

It was almost time for me to get off and I was happy as hell, I was tired and just wanted to jump under the covers. I stayed with my auntie Frankie last night because she'd been on my head about spending time with her. She was bad about throwing a guilt trip on my ass. I didn't mind though, she was the closes person I had to my mom.

I enjoyed being over there while she showed me old pictures and told me plenty of stories about my mama.

I'd been looking in the paper for some cheap and affordable places to live. I was ready to get myself stable and give Amaris back her privacy. Honestly, though, I was a little scared to be living out on my own. I haven't told anybody, but for the last few weeks, I'd been getting some crazy fucking calls and text messages. It's always from an unknown number or a number from those untraceable apps. On top of that, I swear it feels like I'm being watched.

Leaving work, I always made sure to walk out with a group of people and at least one male. After I finally clocked out, I decided to go upstairs to check on Amaris. When I got up there, I walked by a group of catty ass nurses, and I could have sworn I heard them hoes say some dumb shit about my fam. Lord knows I need this job, but they had me bent.

I stood there for a minute just to see if I was imagining shit. When I heard them continue to talk about her I had to check a bitch.

"Y'all talking about Amaris, I was just curious?"

"Yeah, but why are you in our conversation?" this buck tooth ass nurse said.

As I was about to read this hoe, cuzzo walked up. She knew by the look on my face I was about to go the fuck in.

"What you doing up here, I was just about to text you?" Amaris said walking up with her stuff.

It looked like she was getting off, so I'm glad I came up here, I forgot her car was in the shop.

"I came to see if you needed anything before I headed home, I walked up on these baboon looking ass bitches talking shit about you?"

"Girl these mad ass bitches stay talking shit but won't never say a damn thing to my face, they know better. Y'all got something to get off ya chest?" Maris looked at them dead in the eyes and waited, of course, it was nothing but silence.

I can't stand females that were quick to talk shit about somebody behind their back but can't say the shit out loud to the woman's face. Like damn lil' bitch, get that shit off your chest.

We didn't give these hoes any more time, shit it was time to get the fuck out of here. I've been here since seven this morning, here it is twelve hours later, and all I wanted was some good ass food and the T.V. Shit, I don't know how Amaris does it, she was supposed to work sixteen hours today.

Walking to the car that feeling of being watched came over me again. I looked around but didn't see anything.

"Girl, why in the hell you looking around like you fucking crazy. Your ass making me fucking paranoid." She started laughing but if she only knew.

I really debated on if I wanted to tell her or not because I knew just how damn crazy my family is. Being that she started texting on her phone, I thought she would forget all about it. I wasn't that fucking lucky though. She put her phone in her scrubs and started back with her damn interrogation.

"So, what's up, what's got you so shook? Don't even think about lying either."

"I don't know Maris, the shit could really be all in my head, but I swear I feel like somebody is watching me." I took my eyes off the road for a quick second to look at her, I wanted to see what her reaction was gonna be.

"Why would you not say anything, especially since you know that punk ass nigga Draego probably wondering where your ass is at."

"I don't know, I guess I figured there is no way he could track me down. I changed my number so he couldn't contact me."

"Bitch, stop being stupid. You act like you ain't never talk to his stupid ass about your family, and if he really wants to find you, niggas have their ways. You need to just make sure you keep your eyes open at all times and make sure we always know where your ass is going. I'm definitely telling Majik and nem."

Driving home, I thought about what she said, and she was right. If he really wanted to find me, it wouldn't be that damn hard. I guess I wished he wouldn't give a fuck enough to track me down.

I must have for real been in a zone 'cause before I knew it, we were already pulling up to Amaris' apartment. I loved the hell out of this condo, I wished like hell I could afford one over this way.

By the time we got in, and I changed out of my scrubs, there was a knock on the door. I knew it wasn't anybody for me, so I stayed my ass in the room, got comfy in my bed, and started catching up on my shows I missed. I heard a knock on my door, I figured it was Maris, so I didn't even bother getting up or saying anything.

"You know it's rude as fuck to just ignore niggas when they come into your spot shawty?"

Peeping over the covers, I looked straight into the eyes Majik's fine ass. It was like this nigga was imperfectly perfect. He stared back at me stroking the lil' hairs on his chin. Every single time I saw him, he did the same exact thing. He had a way of looking at you like he was looking through your soul.

Walking further into my room, he propped on my dresser, making himself comfortable. Just looking at this man was making a bitch wet.

"Ummm can I help you? I don't remember inviting you in my room." I tried my best to give his ass attitude.

"I've never needed an invited to be in a broad's room, and I tend to do what the fuck I wanna do." Crossing his legs at the foot with his arms crossed over his chest, he continued looking over at me with that sexy ass smirk on his face.

The whole time he'd been in my room, I noticed his phone blowing up. Whoever was calling him was apparently desperate to get him on the fucking line. It had to be a bitch calling him, ain't no way a nigga calling another man like that. I know 'cause I used to call Draego ass like that often.

"Whatever, what can I help you with? Anyway, don't you think you need to answer your phone instead bothering me, somebody really tryna get in touch with you?"

"Why you worried about my line shawty? You must want to be on it?"

"How can I help you sir Majik?" I needed to hurry up and get him up out my room 'cause I'm liable to ride the fuck outta his face.

"I need all the info on this ex-nigga of yours. I don't wanna hear no bullshit ass excuse, just give me the info I need."

Oh shit, did this nigga just check me?

This nigga drilled me for at least thirty minutes, I gave him all the info he needed though. I don't know what he planned on doing, but whatever it was, I hope it kept me safe. I have no idea if it was Draego for real calling me. He didn't wanna do shit but cheat and beat my fucking ass, so I don't know why he would want me back.

Once we were done with our conversation about the fuck boy, I got up and joined everybody in the living room. The shit was mad awkward cause Draiven was trying his best to get Ahnais' attention. She was feeding his ass with a long-handled spoon. His ass was over there begging like Keith Sweat.

"Omg, y'all let's go out and do something tonight. It's Friday night, and I'm off for the next four days. Let's go turn the fuck up somewhere?"

Just thirty minutes ago Amaris' ass was talking about how tired she was, now she tryna go shake her ass, ole confused ass bitch.

"Shit I'm down with it," Lenyx said texting on his phone looking mad as hell.

After everybody agreed on going out, I gave in and said the hell with it. I might as well go have some fun. I haven't really been out since I first got to Atlanta.

"Let me call mama and make sure Yanni good first."

"I just left from over there before we came thru." Draiven giving her, the puppy dog look said.

She didn't respond to him and got up and went to the back. She always kept clothes here, so she probably was going to find something to wear.

"You need to wear something sexy for me. I like my lady looking sexy sometimes."

I don't know why Majik chose this day to fuck with me. A bitch ain't had no dick in a good minute and he playing and shit. I know he got a bitch at home, so I was not about to entertain his ass though.

He was looking at me smirking, so I decided to fuck with him. Looking behind me and side to side, I pretended like I didn't know who he was talking to.

"Y'all need to get ya boy some help, that nigga in here talking to invisible people and shit," I said addressing Lenyx and Draiven. "You do know they got medicine for that shit right Majik? Don't go out like that, you too fine to be up in a nut house."

"So, you been checking a nigga out huh? I knew yo' ass wanted me.

"Dude please, ain't nobody checking for you but that crazy ass baby mama I hear you got on your hands."

We went back and forth flirting and throwing jokes at each other. I wouldn't mind being with a man like Majik. He was most definitely fine as hell, a thug ass gentleman, he was financially stable, and from what I can tell, he isn't a fuck boy.

When the guys left, I jumped up to see what I was going to

wear. I wasn't ready to be in another relationship, but that didn't mean I couldn't get some dick. I needed to turn a few heads tonight, and I planned on doing just that. Majik said dress sexy, it just wasn't gonna be for his ass.

I pulled out this bad ass black bandage dress with the low dip and back out. I loved this dress when I tried it on, it showed the little bit of ass that I had. I've never had the video vixen's ass, but I had just enough to have niggas looking.

After getting out of the shower, I lotioned up and sprayed myself with the best smelling shit I had, I was a determined bitch tonight. I had a nice ass twenty-six-inch lace front install that looked like it had grown straight from my roots. I didn't have to do anything but touch it up a little bit after I had gotten done with my make-up.

Once I was done getting dressed, I looked in the mirror and almost wanted to fuck myself. I was looking just that damn good.

My cousins and I decided to ride together since Ahnais was already at the house and she'd more than likely be staying the night. We rolled a few lil' joints and poured up a shot of Goose before we headed out. It ain't nothing like pregaming before going out.

We valeted and walked straight to the front. Let them tell it, they were never standing in a line. It was a good thing that everybody knew who Draiven's ole lady was. I see it was a few perks to knowing their ass and I wasn't complaining at all. I was looking way too damn good to be standing in anybody's line.

On the way up to the VIP section, we were getting stopped

by damn near every man in our path. Some were fine as hell, and some looked like they mama shitted them out.

I decided to dance a little before I joined the others. I'd had me a few drinks, and I was feeling nice. The DJ was playing all my shit, and I was lit like a muthafucka. I was too through when he played *Booty* by Blac Youngsta. I didn't like some of the lyrics, but for some reason, I still loved the song.

While I was twerking my ass and fucking shit up like I was a stripper, I felt somebody come behind me tryna get a dance. I was glad the song had just ended 'cause I hated dancing with niggas without knowing what they looked like. You wasn't bout to be no ugly ass nigga beind me.

As I started walking off of the dance floor this Lil Boosie looking ass nigga started pulling on my arm tryna get my number. He had some fucking nerve with his breath smelling like hot garbage, and that's putting it mildly. I tried letting his ass down easy, but he wasn't getting it. I was so not in the mood for this.

"So shawty, you for real not tryna give me yo' number?"

"I'm good, thank you though," I said for the last time and walked away. This ugly nigga made the mistake of grabbing my wrist.

"Look don't put your fucking hands on me, you got me fucked up!" I said snatching away from him.

"You think you fucking better than me or something? You stuck up bitches get on my fucking nerves. A nigga tryna to be nice to you bitches and y'all don't know how to fucking act."

I could tell by the look in his eyes, that if we were alone, he would have probably really done something to me. His ugly ass had the nerve to have his face all frowned up and shit. As ugly as he is, he didn't need to fuck his face up no more than it already was.

I see how this night was gonna go, and I wasn't here for this stupid shit. I couldn't even enjoy a night out without the extra nonsense.

MAJIK

I was kicking shit with the homie Joc when I looked down at the dance floor and saw that fuck ass nigga grabbing up on Nautica. A nigga just wanted to chill for one night without having to fuck somebody up. I jumped up and left his ass talking to his got damn self.

I could see it in this muthafuckas posture he was on some stupid shit. I made it over to ole girl before he was able to do anything.

I stepped in between the two and looked at that clown ass fool with my hands on my heat.

"We got a problem nigga?"

"Not shit that concerns your punk ass." This nigga said and spit towards my shoe.

See, niggas always tryna show out and shit. I was just gonna beat his ass or some shit, now he was about to meet the man that created his ugly ass. He had to be some type of creature, what normal nigga just spits for no damn reason.

I wasn't the type of man to use many words, I was all action. Conversing with a nigga you know you about to kill was a waste of time and I damn sho' didn't like my time to be wasted.

Before he could form his next thought, I punched his ass in the throat and slammed his face into my knee. He couldn't even drop his first drip of blood on the floor before my niggas carried his ass out. I didn't have to speak or give orders, they knew what the fuck to do.

"Bring yo' ass up here to our VIP, yo' ass shouldn't have been down here alone any got damn way."

"Nigga you ain't my fuckin daddy, I don't even know his ass!"

I was just about sick of her damn mouth. She 'bout to make me stick something in it so she could shut her smart mouth ass the fuck up.

"Shawty, do you ever shut the hell up? That shit was cute at first, now it's just fucking annoying man. Did you forget niggas may be after your stubborn ass?"

If she wanted to get her ass killed by that nigga that shit is on her. I'm not about to babysit her ass if she didn't wanna fucking listen. Fuck that shit, I could be looking for some more pussy to get into tonight.

I left her standing right there where she was and took my ass back to where the fuck I was. Once I had a bottle of Ace of Spades brought to our section, I rolled a fat ass blunt and chilled out. I still kept my eyes open for any bullshit.

Out the corner of my eyes, I saw Nautica walking up on me looking like she wanted to say something. I wasn't about to make shit easy for her ass, she know she was wrong as hell for that stunt she pulled. I know I was gonna make her ass mine, so she needed to learn early on how to let a man lead. She been dealing with busta ass niggas for too long and didn't know when she was in the presence of a fucking king.

"So ummm I'm sorry for um, what happened downstairs," I could tell her ass wasn't used to apologizing cause that apology sucked.

I wanted to make her sweat for a little while longer, so I just looked at her, nodded, and continued smoking my blunt.

"I see you aren't gonna make this easy for me?" sitting down next to me, she tried to give me the damn puppy dog eyes.

The more I ignored her, the more she tried to hold a conversation with me. By the time I was on my second blunt, I was beginning to become bored.

"You gotta tighten up ma. I know you used to dealing with sucka ass niggas and shit, but you need to realize when a real mufucka tryna lead you."

I said what I had to say about the situation and let it be that. I was not about to continue going on about the same shit over and over again.

Sitting here smoking and drinking with shawty, we had a pretty good convo going on. I could tell she wasn't just a pretty face, she wanted shit out of life. The music was loud as hell and folks was everywhere, but shit it felt like it was just us in the room, that's just how much we was vibin'.

"So, when you gonna let a nigga take you out on some real shit?" we were sitting so close together, she was damn near in my lap. I lifted her legs over mine and started rubbing my hands through her hair.

"I'm supposed to let you take me out, and you got female at home? Shit, I'm tryna get away from drama and bullshit, not add to It." she looked at me with that pretty ass smile of hers and looking at her in the eyes, I wanted to drop this dick off in her right here.

I ain't ever had a female in my life that had my dick hard just from looking at her ass. She got the game all the way twisted if she thinks she ain't bout to be mine. Soon I won't have to worry about her using me having a woman as an excuse. I was working hard to get rid of my baby mama.

I'd just gotten CoCo a house built so my baby girl could have a stable home and didn't have to worry about having a roof over her head. I was gonna make sure the bills were paid, and Majesti had whatever she needed, but that is where it'll end for me. I'm sure Co think I'mma be supporting her ass, that shit damn sure ain't about to happen though.

"See there you go speaking and worrying about some irrele-vant ass shit ma."

I could tell she was about to let some fly shit pop out of her mouth but didn't get the chance. It seemed like the whole damn club was looking in our direction, but, it was just the nosey mufuckas close to us.

"What the fuck is this shit Majik?" CoCo said walking up with a deep mug on her face. Now I know why these niggas was in here being nosey as hell, at least one of their asses could have warned me this bitch was rolling up on me, not that I really gave a damn.

CoCo knew I wasn't with all that acting stupid and shit in public and she for damn sure know I ain't bout to answer to a bitch ass thing.

I waited for her to finish her show while looking at her like she was stupid.

"So, you just gonna sit there looking fucking stupid and not fucking answer me? Who the fuck is this bitch Majik?"

"Who the fuck you calling a bitch?"

Nautica swung her legs off me with the quickness trying to get up. I had to hurry up and dead that shit. I was the most feared nigga out here in these streets making more money then I knew what to do with, the last thing I needed was extra attention on me.

The less heat I had on me, the better, I always made sure to keep it that way.

She was rapidly bouncing her leg and biting her lip, mad as hell. I was never the type of man that was okay with a bunch of women out here in the streets fighting over him. That shit was classless.

Out the corner of my eye, I could see Ahnais and Amaris approaching us, and by the look on their faces, I already knew they were on some good bullshit. I leaned over towards Nautica's ear and told her to chill out and let me handle this shit. I ended up whispering a few other things that made her lil' ass blush.

Shit, I got caught up flirting with Nautica's ass that I forgot just that quick that CoCo was in my face with this goofy ass shit.

"You not about to fucking sit here and muthafuckin disrespect me Majik!" she yelled out and mushed me in the forehead with her finger. Her ghetto ass nails were so long, the bitch fucked around and scratched my forehead.

I slowly stood up while checking out my head, I checked to see if I was bleeding or not. That shit was burning like hell. I'm a light, bright ass nigga, she better hope that shit don't leave a fucking mark on me. Shit, Ima pretty boy ass thug. I could see it in her eyes, she knows she done fucked up bad. I was raised not to hit women, but I was also told, you put your hands on me, and I had every right to knock your head off your shoulders.

I guess she figured since we were in a room full of people that I wouldn't do anything to her, so she was still tryna save face in front of her home girls.

Walking towards her, I was getting madder and madder. I was just gonna choke her ass up, now she bout two seconds to meeting her maker.

"You think you the shit, we gonna see how hard yo' ass is when you getting raped behind them bars. Majesti gonna be calling another nigga daddy!" I couldn't stand a bitch that don't know when to just shut the fuck up.

I made it over to her ass before she could even form her next sentence. Choking her ass up, I lifted her clean off her feet with one hand.

"Bitch, who the fuck you think you talking to, huh? Do you

know who the fuck I am hoe?" I had spit flying out my mouth I was so muthafuckin pissed off.

The shit that just came out her mouth, she ain't gonna need that fuckin house I just got. I see her and her cousin bout to die together. Both of these hoes done came out their mouths bout the law and I ain't with that threatening shit.

Before I knew it, I had done blacked out and all I saw was red.

"Bro, come on, let that bitch go. You 'bout to kill her ass." Lenyx said while trying to pry my hands from around her throat.

"Nah this bitch got so much to say, let's see if her ass can talk now. I'm sick of these hoes stepping outta line." I said as I squeezed her neck tighter. I could see the fear in her eyes and that shit gave me a hard-on.

"Cuz I feel you, but not here. We got too many eyes on us right now. Man chill out, look at Nautica, shorty ain't feeling what you doing."

I didn't want to hear that shit Lenyx was spitting, but I knew cuz was speaking some real shit. I glanced over at Nautica, and I could see her trembling. It hit me that fast that shawty must have been thinking of the shit she had been through with that fuck nigga.

All it took was one look on her pretty ass face, and I dropped that bitch on the ground like a sack of fucking potatoes. I watched CoCo closely as she held her neck while struggling to breathe. I wished the bitch would have fucked died, so I didn't have to deal with her ass anymore. This muthafucka has been testing me lately, and it was time for me to show her that I didn't give a fuck about her and her ass was disposable.

Walking back towards Nautica, I needed to see where shawty head was at. I didn't give a damn about nothing else at the moment. All the nosey ass niggas in this got damn club finally went back to minding their fucking business.

"Aye, I just wanna for real apologize for that shit you just saw. That ain't the type of nigga I am. I don't deal well with muthafuckas threatening my freedom, but that was still my bad." I went to grab her hand, and I noticed her flinching. "You good?"

Whatever that nigga put her through had her head gone for real. She acting like I just bodied the hoe.

"Umm yeah, I'm fine. I think it's time for me to call it a night though. You've been in two altercations because of me, I think I might be bad luck."

She tried to lighten up the mood, but I could still tell she wasn't feeling my ass right now. I was just gonna have to work hard and showing her the type of man I really am. I've never been the type of man to put my hands on a woman.

I walked the ladies to the car while listening to them go on and on about what they would do to CoCo, I personally didn't wanna hear that back and forth shit. I was more concerned with the shit I needed to do.

After making sure they were safely in the car and on their way, I headed back inside. I got word on where my baby mama went, and I made my way in her direction.

I posted up by the women's bathrooms waiting for this loud trout mouth ass bitch to walk up out of there. I know she wasn't doing nothing but in there talking shit and fixing her bargain buy ass hair. I tried to choke every track she had out her muthafuckin head.

"I bet you that nigga won't see my damn daughter no mo-"

After I just snatched this hoe up, she still had the audacity to be talking shit and trying a nigga. She had the whole world fucked up if she thought she was about to keep my baby girl away from me.

She didn't even finish her sentence once she realized she done fucked up yet again.

"So, I see you haven't learned your lesson huh CoCo? Come take a ride wit me right quick."

For the second time in less than an hour, I saw in her eyes that she knew she had done fucked up royally.

If I killed her ass tonight, I might as well put myself in the electric chair. I had to be smart about this shit and play it out the right way. One thing a nigga did know though, and that's that I couldn't deal with this bullshit for the rest of my life with her ass.

I'm gonna hate taking away my daughter's mother but shit it's either that bitch or me. I choose me, I'll always choose me.

AMARIS

I was supposed to have introduced Jaysun to the family last night at the club, but I'm glad he wasn't able to make it. Shit went left quick as hell. Majik need to hurry up and do something about his stupid ass baby mama. That hoe don't do shit but spend his money and cause fucking trouble. Her ass don't ever have Majesti.

Me and Jaysun been spending a lot of time together and I was starting to have a soft spot for his ass. He had constantly been asking me to meet his daughter, and I turned him down every time. It's not that I didn't want to meet her, I just didn't want to get too attached to her and shit between us fall apart. She already lost her mama and didn't need women coming in and out of her life.

Today we were meeting up at Andretti for a little fun. This will be my first time meeting Destiny face to face. I've talked to her a few times on the phone, but I was still a little nervous. I was bringing Yanni with me since they were about the same age. I hope this little girl had some act right cause Yanni stayed with the shit, her lil' ass wouldn't hesitate to cut up if she needed to.

While we were in the car headed to meet up with them, I was enjoying my one on one conversation with my number one lil' lady. She always kept me entertained with the shit that came out of her mouth.

"Tee Tee, it's this one girl in my class, and I swear she aggy. Every day she like 'Ayanni you so pretty. I'm like umm yeah thank you. She gon' have the nerve to say so you not gonna say it back. I looked at her and said umm did I say it?"

"Butterball why didn't you say it back?" I couldn't help but laugh at this crazy ass girl.

"Cause Tee, y'all told me if I didn't have anything nice to say not to say nothing at all. I couldn't lie to her."

I always took advantage of the time I spent with my niece. She will never feel like she isn't loved. I didn't go a day without speaking to her and letting her know that I loved her.

We talked and cut up all the way there, by the time we got there, I had laughed so hard my stomach was hurting. Before we went inside, I had to warn Yanni to watch what she says towards Destiny. I was afraid once she saw her without hair that she would speak before she thought.

Walking inside I was already bout to turn around and go home. It was way too many fucking kids running round. These disrespectful as kids didn't have any manners either, they running into folks and looking you up and down like you in the wrong.

I spotted Jaysun and made my way over to him. I felt myself smiling, and of course, Yanni noticed it before I could stop it.

"Tee Tee and Jaysun sitting in the tree, K.I.S.S.I.N.G, first comes love, then comes marriage, then comes Tee Tee with the baby carriage." This lil' girl was singing and doing the milly rock in the middle of the floor.

She is so got damn embarrassing sometimes. I pulled up to the booth they were sitting in.

"It's about time, I thought you was gonna stand a nigga up." He sat pulling the hairs on his chin, smirking with them pretty ass white teeth of his.

"Stop it, I told you I was coming."

"Destiny this is daddy's friend Amaris. Amaris, this is my baby girl Destiny."

"Hello gorgeous, it's nice to finally meet you," I said giving her a hug. I figured shaking her hands was a little too formal.

Seeing this little girl up close and personal didn't do her beauty justice. Even with the loss of her hair, she was still so beautiful. She had the prettiest doe-shaped eyes with a cinnamon brown complexion. She spoke back to me, but I could tell she was really shy even though I had spoken to her a few times before by phone.

"Everyone this is my niece Ayanni. Yanni this is Jaysun and his daughter Destiny."

"Umm yeah, yeah, hey and all that. That's enough of all the

speaking. Destiny, I don't know bout you, but wouldn't you rather go play with me?"

This lil' heffa's mouth, she will make a sane person lose their mind. Jaysun was getting a kick out of the shit that was coming out of her mouth. Once he got to know her a little better and was around her more, I'm going to see if he thought the shit was still so damn cute.

It seemed like Destiny and Yanni had known each other all their lives. They were immediately drawn to each other and was having the time of their lives together. That alone spoke volumes because my niece was just like her Tee Tee. We didn't like no damn body.

"I guess they just forgot about us. So how did Destiny's appointment go?"

I probably should have picked another subject to speak on. I could see the sadness come upon his face. The last thing I wanted to do was cause him any sadness.

"Fuck ass doctor told me that not only is her cancer spreading but she has a tumor now that's growing pretty fast. I ain't tryna hear that shit though."

While keeping our eyes on the girls, we sat back and talked and just enjoyed some time together. About thirty minutes later, I saw the girls walking up, and I could tell that something was wrong. Not only was Destiny looking a little weak, but I could also tell that she had been crying or on the verge.

"What's wrong with Destiny," I asked Yanni. Before she could even answer me, I looked at Destiny to see if I could get some answers out of her. "Are you okay sweetie, what's wrong?"

"Tee Tee, this stupid girl was over there making fun of Destiny because she don't have hair. It made her sad, so I punched her in the face. We wasn't bothering anybody. Des didn't feel good, so we were just trying to sit down. She said she was going to get her mama, but I told Destiny not to worry cause you would beat that lady's ass, won't you Tee Tee?"

Yanni literally gave me a full explanation all in less than a minute. I don't even think her ass took a breath in between words.

"Ayanni, you better watch your got damn mouth!" I tried hard to get on to her and be serious, but I started laughing before I could finish my sentence.

Jaysun was sitting across from me laughing too, and that didn't help at all.

"Why did you hit her? Why couldn't you have just told her it wasn't nice or something?" I needed to make sure she understood that she can't just go around hitting people. I would never tell her not to defend herself though.

"She is my best friend, and she hurt her feelings, so I hurt her face." she shrugged her shoulders like it was no big deal. It made sense to her, so I guess that is all that mattered.

This ghetto ass woman dressed like she was going to the club walked up on us with her face turned up. I knew this was the little girl's mother that Yanni smacked up. Why this bitch was dressed like this around these kids, I had no clue.

I know my niece was in the wrong, but so was her daughter, so she better come at me like she got some sense.

By the way this woman was standing there smacking her

gum with her hand on her hip, I knew this was about to go all the south.

"Umm is dis your lil' girl?

You gotta be damn kidding me? Do this bitch really got gold teeth in her mouth?

"She's my niece, is there a problem?" I was about to play as dumb as this bitch actually is.

"Yeah Issa problem, she fucking put her hands on my damn child!"

This hoe was tryna get loud. She was being so fucking extra she caused a scene and a crowd of people formed around us. Didn't Sha-Nae-Nae teach these hoodrat ass hoes how to be a lady?

"Excuse me Miss, but there ain't no need for you to be yelling and shit. Did your precious daughter tell you what she did? Now I don't condone what she did to your daughter at all, and I will handle it." In order for this to end with me not slapping this bitch, I tried to speak to her calm and with control.

We tried to explain what transpired between the girls. I was hoping that once she realized that her daughter was making fun of a child that has cancer, she would understand why Yanni did what she did and get onto her child.

Of course, that would be like too much right. This food stamp, section eight recipient ass hoe still wanted to pop off.

"Bitch, I don't give a fuck what Taequanna did, if that lil' bitch touches my child again, it's gonna be a problem, I fight kids about mine."

Did this funky breath bitch just threaten my baby? Amaris

don't beat her ass, you don't want the girls to think that is how you suppose to solve things. Amaris beat the fuck outta her, she threatened your niece.

I was having an internal conflict with myself on how I wanted to handle this. It didn't take too long for me to make a choice once I saw her drop her cheap ass City Trend purse.

Stepping a few steps forward, gold mouth swung on me. She fucked up when she didn't keep swinging.

I punched her in the throat and twice in her face before she had even realized that she was getting her ass beat the fuck up. I wasn't bout to play with her ass. She wanted this ass whooping so got dammit I was giving it to her. This bitch was going to be dreaming about these hits as I monkey stomped this hoe in the face.

I had to push Yanni out the way, her ass done jumped in and kicked the bitch in the side. My heart swelled with pride on the inside. Seeing Destiny crying and looking hella pale out the corner of my eye is the only thing that made me stop.

Jerking away from Jaysun, I ran over to Destiny to make sure she was okay. I hope she didn't think I was this ratchet ass female that her daddy was tryna date. I definitely didn't want to give off that impression.

"Sweetie are you okay? I'm so sorry."

Her cries were making me feel worse than I already did. She had a treatment today and didn't need to get herself overworked. Her dad was doing everything in his power to get her to calm down.

"This is all my fault, if I hadn't been sick, this never would have happened. I don't want y'all to get in trouble because of me."

I sat her on my lap and let her know everything would be okay. I assured her that none of this was on her.

Somebody had called the police, and when they walked in, this cunt bitch tried to give an award-winning performance. I wasn't gonna move or say shit until them muthafuckas came to me.

They finally made it over to me, I didn't really have to say much. Patrons that witness the ordeal and recorded the shit had my back. Even though she got her ass beat, she was still charged with assault since she threw the first lick.

The girls were ready to go, and we were all over it.

"Why don't y'all come back to the house with us, I mean if you don't have anything else to do," Jaysun suggested and thinking about it, I wasn't ready to end our time together, so I agreed.

I ran to the store and grabbed a shit load of snacks and a few movies. I was gonna turn this into a movie night. By the time we made it to his house, he was getting Destiny settled. She was still a little fatigued and didn't have much energy. It was crazy how one minute she was fine, and within an hour everything changed.

We put Jaysun out of the room, and I helped get her together for the night. Laying her down on the couch, Yanni got one of her thick blankets and laid next to her holding her hand.

The scene before me was so beautiful, I had to take a picture of it. Looking at the two of them, no one would ever guess that they had just met each other a few hours ago. They look like they had been friends all their lives.

I snuggled up next to Jaysun, and for the first time in a long time, I was actually completely letting my guard down with a man.

AHNAIS

*J*t's been about two months, and shit between Draiven and I were still fucked up. We finally sat down, and he told me everything that happened. He claimed he may have been drugged, but I don't know if I believe that shit or not. I have to say, that nigga ain't never done anything to make me think he was unfaithful in the past.

He promised that he was going to fix us, I hope he can hold up to that promise because I don't know how much more of this bullshit with him I was going to be able to take. He been doing everything he possibly can though and I have to give him his props on that.

He could be out here in the clubs and fucking everything moving, I mean he could, but that would just put his ass in danger 'cause I would for sure try to kill ass.

I've been trying to get some information on this Tatiana hoe, but it seems like this hoe just came out of thin air. That shit was suspicious. I was determined to get down to the bottom of this shit, and I was going to do the shit sooner than later. I was ready for shit to get back to normal. I was sick of Yanni asking me when her daddy was gonna be able to come home. I think his ass was putting her up to asking me that shit.

I was just getting off of work and shit felt weird. Looking around in the parking lot, I notice a dark tinted windowed van park towards the back. That shit was a total red flag. I made my way back into the pharmacy and went into my office quickly, locking the door behind me.

I pulled out my phone and hurried up and called Draiven. It took a few rings for him to answer and I was grateful. Today was not the day for him to go missing.

"What's up bae, you off work yet?" he asked blowing smoke in the phone. This nigga can't go two seconds without smoking.

"Yeah, I was walking to the car and shit didn't seem right Drae. On top of that, it's a dark-colored van parked out there, and the shit seems hella out of place." I told him, cutting right to the chase.

"Where are you Ahnais?" he asked sounding alarmed. That alone had me on edge now. He's never been the type of person to get high strung about something. He was always the laid-back type of guy.

"I came back in the building, I'm in my office now. What's wrong Draiven, what the hell is going on?"

"Nothing man chill out, just stay in there. I'm on the way up there. Calm yo' ass down and don't hang up this phone."

"How the hell am I supposed to calm down and you won't tell me what's going on. That's why we fucked up now cause yo' ass wanna keep secrets and shit!"

"Aye, shut yo' ass up man, now ain't the time for you to be spitting that dumb shit."

"Whatever Drae, how far are you? I'm tired and ready to get my baby and go home." I sighed and leaned back in my chair.

"You might as well get untired, don't forget we supposed to go out with baby girl tonight." I'm surprised he even remembered that we had plans tonight, shit I damn near forgot my damn self.

"Do you think that is a good idea? We don't know who that is outside or what's going on."

"Shut the fuck up with that dumb shit man. You done said bout four stupid ass things since we been on the phone. Fuck is wrong wit you Shawty?"

"What you mea-" this nigga cut me off and didn't even let me finish my damn sentence. That is some rude ass shit.

"I'm pulling up, save that shit you bout to say. I'm sure it's some more fucked up shit."

He hung up on me, and I was tempted to smack the fuck out his ass when he walked up in here. He knows I can't stand to be hung up on. That is some rude ass shit.

I heard him trying to turn the doorknob, but it was locked. I started to be spiteful and leave his ass out there knocking, but I was too tired and was just ready to get home.

I didn't open the door though until I knew for sure, it was him on the other side. I gathered up all my stuff and followed him back out to my car. I glanced over to where the van was sitting and saw two men getting thrown in the back. I guess it's safe to say, them niggas got caught slipping.

"Give me yo' car keys babe" I reached into my purse wondering how the hell he got up here in the first place.

"Where the hell is your car at and how the hell did you even get up here?" I handed him the keys and got my ass in slamming the door.

I didn't have a valid reason to be mad though, I know I was tripping for no reason.

"Aye, shawty tell the truth, yo' ass use to ride the short yellow bus when you was a kid, didn't you? It's that or you been dipping in them patient's medications. Yo' ass crazy as fuck, for real man."

"Fuck you Draiven, I ain't slow or crazy. You think yo' ass slick."

I guess he called himself ignoring me because he didn't give me a response. It's okay, I was tired of the back and forth bull-shit anyway. I was wondering where he was going because it was the opposite direction of my mama's house. He knows we needed to go pick up Yanni or she'd be blowing up both of our phones.

I'd been scrolling through Facebook looking at all the dumb ass post these bitches be putting up. It's crazy how they put up all their business then complain when people up in their mix.

Before long we were pulling up to the house we shared together, and I was wondering why the hell we were here.

"Get out and come on Ahnais!" he turned the car off, got out the car and slammed the door shut. I have no idea what the fuck is wrong with this nigga just that damn quick.

Mentally preparing myself for whatever bullshit this nigga was on, I took my time getting out the car and going inside.

Since I didn't see him nowhere in sight, I took my ass in the kitchen to get me something to snack on. Grabbing my phone out of my back pocket, I needed to see who was blowing my shit up. I was getting messages coming in back to back.

Yanni Boo: mama where you at?

Maris: Bitttccchhh I gotta tell you bout the shit that happened last night

Yanni Boo: where my daddy at? I'm ready to go home mama, nana in a bad mood. I think it's that time of her month

Me: I'll be there in a few Yanni. I'm with daddy

Me: I'll call you in a few Maris. What the hell is wrong with mama? Yanni said she was in a bad mood.

I grabbed my apple and headed to the living room to wait for Draiven. As I turned around, I bumped right into him, and he scared the fuck out of me.

"Ahhhh fuck, you fucking scared me! Why the hell you sneaking up on me?"

"Shut the fuck up Ahnais"

He pushed me backward up against the kitchen counter while kissing me on the neck. Sucking on my earlobe, he started unbuckling and removing my slacks. I wasn't sure if I was up for what I knew was about to happen, but him sucking on my neck was making all my good sense go out the window. He knew damn well that was my fucking spot.

"Wha wha what are you doing Draiven?"

He was fingering me so damn good I could barely form a damn sentence. I don't know why some women said they didn't like to be fingered, shit was damn near the best feeling in the world.

"Bout to give you this dick, you been on some good bullshit lately."

In one quick motion, my thong and pants were pulled off, and I was lifted on the kitchen island. Pushing my head down, he started licking my pussy from behind. Sticking his tongue in as far as it could go, I damn near came from that alone. He licked and sucked on my pussy until the bud was swollen and I had come at least five times.

Turning me towards him and sitting me up, he tongued me down while rubbing his hand up and down my pussy. With the other hand, I felt him unbuckling his belt and pulling out his dick.

I hope he can fix this relationship and get his shit together, 'cause his big ass dick is one thing I'll definitely miss. This man walking around with this big ass horse Safaree dick.

When he put his dick inside me all I could do was silently thank the man above. It felt so got damn good. He fucked me on that counter like he was proving a point.

"Ohhhhhh shit, Draeeeeee. Ohhhh my goodddd!"

"Yeah, talk that shit you was spitting earlier now."

I couldn't say shit 'cause this nigga had me seeing fucking stars and speaking in tongues.

This nigga slid my ass off the counter while he had his dick still inside of me. I felt like an extra in the movie *Baby Boy* when ole boy's mama was getting fucked by the Ving Rhames. He was walking us to the living room and still fucking my ass silly.

I had to redeem my damn self, ain't no way I was bout to go out like a lame. He was bout to get this throwback. I jumped out his arm and pushed him down on the couch.

I sat on his lap backward so I could ride his ass cowgirl style. I eased down slowly on that big ass dick of his, I wasn't trying to tear up my insides. I kept slowly moving up and down winding my hips.

"Oooh shit, got dammit girl! This pussy wet as fuck."

Going down all the way, I continued to grind my hips like I was in a Jamaican video. Bending down, I grabbed his ankles and held onto them as I bounced up and down.

"Fuck Draiven, fuck nigga this dick so got damn good. Oooohhhhh shit, babbbyyyyy fuckkkkkkkk!" I couldn't do shit but say the same shit over and over.

"You gonna fix your muthafuckin attitude, huh?" He slid to the edge of the couch and took control. Holding me by my waist, he began pounding that dick in me so hard I damn near felt it coming out my throat.

We fucked all over that damn living room, switching positions, and trying to outdo one another for the next hour. After I'd cum well over six times, he finally released hard in me. I know if I wasn't on birth control that his ass would've just gotten me pregnant.

After that round of sex, I didn't want to do shit but climb up in my bed and take a fucking nap. I was hoping Yanni ass didn't remember we'd told her we were going out tonight, 'cause a bitch didn't feel like doing shit.

Draiven had gone upstairs to the bathroom to get me a wash-cloth, and I dozed off that quick. He smacked me on the ass and woke me up.

"Get yo' ass up, Yanni just called and she ready for us to come get her."

"Dammit, I'm tired, I was damn sho' hoping she didn't remember we had plans."

"You know that shit ain't bout to happen. Baby girl don't forget shit. I'm bout to go get dressed, getcha ass on up. I told her we'd be there soon." He said walking out of the room. Dick just swinging back and forth.

I laid there for about five more minutes, and I willed myself to get up. One thing I would never do in my life is disappoint my baby girl. I finally got myself together and got ready to head out to make her smile.

DRAIVEN

I was a few steps closer to getting my damn family back. Shit has been going a lot smoother since I put that dick in her life. She still ain't talking to a nigga much, but at least she came back home where the fuck she belonged. I was tired of not seeing my baby girl like I wanted to.

Ayanni was starting to question my love for her, and that's some shit I can't have. My daughter would never search for love through another muthafucka when she had a daddy to show her what the shit was.

I was headed to meet up with my homie Kwame. I'd let him know about this shit with Tatiana and had him looking into it. On the phone, it seemed like he had some heavy shit to lay on me and a nigga was ready to hear what the fuck he had to say. I already know I'm killing the bitch, but I wanted to know what the fuck she got going on though.

I was meeting this nigga at *Stats,* a lil' bar downtown cause a nigga for real needed a drink or two. By the time I'd pulled up I was on edge like a muthafucka. When I got in there it was so many niggas standing around, it took me a good lil' minute to find his ass. Once I located that nigga, I was ready to get this shit over with.

"What's up witcha homie?" I dapped him up and sat down in the booth.

As soon as I sat down, the waiter came, and I placed a quick order for some wings and two Coronas.

"Shit I'm straight dawg, out here chasing this money and these bitches. Aye but check this out bruh, you gon' need more than a beer to handle this shit I'm bout to lay on your ass."

This nigga was making me more anxious to know what the fuck he done found out. I hope I didn't have to go to this hoe house tonight and split her shit back.

"Man, if it ain't one thing is a muthafuckin notha'. What's the deal though, lay that shit on me."

"Well first things first, I checked the surveillance cameras at the warehouse that bitch cooking at, and it's a fact that bitch drugged yo' ass. It looks like that grimy hoe been plotting on yo' ass for a minute. The Gatorades you keep in yo' office, she been slipping shit in them bitches. The only reason you ain't get caught slipping sooner, cause it looks like you ain't been in the office long enough to drink one of those bitches."

The more he talked, the more I was getting pissed off. I would sometimes grab one of those damn Gatorades to take home to Yanni. Her ass loved to drink them just as much as I did and some nights a nigga just didn't wanna stop at the store when we were out at the house.

"You gotta be fucking kidding me bruh? I knew that bitch must have drugged me or some shit!" I was so got damn pissed, I was talking louder than I needed to be. I damn sho' didn't need muthafuckas overhearing shit I was speaking on.

"I hear she working for some big-time Italian who got a hard-on for you and yo' family. I'm still digging and waiting for a name."

This shit was blowing my fucking mind man. I don't know who the fuck coming for us, we don't make enemies we make money. We run across a few hating, clown ass niggas every once in a while, but the shit always gets deaded, literally.

I chopped it up with the homie Kwame' for a lil' bit longer and paid him for the information he provided. I made sure I got the video to show that bitch drugged me so I could show Ahnais' ass. Now maybe she let a nigga back in between those legs on a regular.

Once I was through kicking it at *Stats,* I hit up that nigga Majik and let him know I needed to holla at his ass. He needed to be brought in on what I just found out. We suppose to handle some shit tonight with Len anyway, so I could tell both them niggas.

Sending Ahnais a text, I needed her to be up when I got in so we could talk.

Me: Ayee babe, I got some shit I need to put you up on. I need yo' ass to be up when I get there.

My Wife: What is it Draiven? I'm tired and ready to call it a night already.

Me: This is some serious shit man, FR. For once just do what the fuck a nigga asked.

My Wife: who the fuck you talking to Drae?

I wasn't about to keep going back and forth with this damn girl. I flamed up another blunt and made my way towards the spot to meet the fellas. I wanted to get this shit over with as quick as possible so I could take my ass to the crib.

As I rode through the streets of Atlanta, smoking on that good ass gas straight from Mexico, I thought about all the bullshit that had been going on in the last few months. This shit was draining the fuck outta me. All a nigga wanted to do was make this money, take care of my family, and be a good man to my lady. All this extra shit was for the fucking birds.

I pulled up to the crib Majik, and Lenyx used to bust down the groupie ass hoes from around the way. Everybody in Atlanta and surrounding states knew who the fuck we were, it wasn't nothing for us to go somewhere and have a bitch on her knees in a place full of people. Bitches got into fights at the clubs a few times trying to be seen partying with us, shit was crazy. These scum bucket head ass hoes stayed looking for the next come up.

Before I got with Ahnais, all these hoes could do was come up for air and get back down on their knees and finish swallowing this dick. They wasn't getting shit from me but a mouth full of my nut.

I immediately saw a few strippers on the pole doing the damn thing. I couldn't do shit but shake my damn head. I needed to hurry up and get the fuck up out of here. I damn sho' didn't need to get caught out here. I would never hear the end of that shit.

I went searching the house and didn't see neither one of them. I told they ass I was on the way, I hope they wasn't in the room fucking. I didn't have all got damn night.

Both of them niggas walked from the back, smiling like hell with two bitches each. I'm not about to even get into what they asses had just got finished doing.

"Man if y'all don't bring y'all Hugh Heffner wanna be asses on, I got shit to do."

"Nigga pull ya panties out ya ass and drop ya balls." Majik stupid ass said causing the hoes he had walking behind him to snicker.

I threw they ass the did I give you the permission to laugh look. Them hoes scattered off quick like some damn roaches. That was the best thing for them to do at this point.

I kicked it with them niggas for about an hour or so blazing and putting them up on the shit Kwame' put in my ear. It was time for a nigga to head home and deal with this shit with Ahnais. I can guarantee her ass didn't do what the fuck I asked her to do. That's exactly why my ass wasn't in no hurry to get to the crib. After I took her this got damn tape, she better drop the attitude and let shit get back to normal.

LENYX

I was finally getting rid of my problem tonight. I was glad as fuck too, 'cause I didn't know how much longer I was gonna be able to keep pretending. Tori thought she really got over on a nigga because of what she said. I had something for that ass though, and she was bout to get it. I was bout to treat this hoe like a death row inmate, she was bout to have a bomb ass last meal and everything.

It had been about two months since she pulled that fuck shit and I been counting down the days since. I was bout to go and holla at Majik to make sure shit was set up the way it needed to go.

Amaris introduced us to her new nigga, and that bullshit had me in my feelings. I was pissed off because she had the fucking nerve to be flaunting her ass around here happy and my relationship went up in smoke. I was also pissed off because I chose the wrong bitch to settle down with. I had the perfect chance to settle down with a good, down ass female like Amaris. Now I done let another clown ass nigga snatch her the fuck up. Fuck that nigga.

Once I was done with Majik, I needed to go holla at my pops. I needed to start spending more time with his old ass, that nigga ain't getting no damn younger. He wasn't bout to do shit but get on my ass about letting Maris' ass slip away.

It didn't take me no time to make it to my people's house. I used the spare key that I had and walked my ass right in. I wasn't in the mood to be ringing doorbells and shit. I found that nigga in his man cave playing *Madden 2K18*, online talking shit as usual, and smoking on some good ass shit.

"Got damn my nigga, do yo' ass always gotta be somewhere being fucking loud and shit. I coulda been somebody coming to rob ya ass nigga." I said sitting down getting comfortable.

I grabbed the other controller 'cause I already know I was bout to bust this nigga's ass right quick. It wasn't nothing for my ass to get on that damn game and show the fuck out.

"Nigga I stay ready fuck you mean." Pulling out his pistol from under his leg, he placed it in front of him on the table.

This nigga even had the got damn safety off already.

"Aight, yo' ass gonna shoot yo' muthafuckin leg off nigga. Then we gonna call yo' ass Lieutenant Dan. Ole Forrest Gump face ahh" This damn weed was so damn good and potent, my ass was laughing like the shit was really funny.

We ran a few games, and I was getting pissed cause this nigga had one up on me. If I don't win this last game, I'mma be losing five stacks. That shit ain't nothing to a boss nigga though, but I damn sho' didn't wanna hear the shit from his ass if he won.

Once the game was over and I paid the nigga the lil' chump change he won, it was time to get down to the real ass reason I was here.

"So what's the plan for this bum ass bitch, Cuz?"

"Ain't no plan, we just gonna kill the bitch. Take the hoe out to eat or some shit. Make sure it's somewhere that will get you on camera. I already know that until I take care of CoCo's ass, she's not gonna let the shit go that the hoe is missing."

"That's what I'm afraid of, I don't need them folks, sniffing around our shit, for no reason at all."

"Her ass ain't gonna be amongst the living too much longer either. I hate to do that shit to my baby girl, but that bitch been threatening my freedom a little too much for my liking."

That was some hard shit to have to do. I'm glad it wasn't me. I don't know if I could make that choice. I doubt I would be able to take my kid's mother away from them. On the other hand though, it ain't like the bitch is mother of the year. Her ass don't ever have my damn niece. She always putting Maj off on some damn body.

"Aight fool, I'm up outta here. Meet me at the spot, I'll send you a text when I'm on the way."

I sent Torrie a text to go ahead and meet me at the restaurant we were eating at tonight. I planned this shit out as perfect as I could. I wanted to make sure her ass was seen getting in her own shit tonight.

She made it there before I did and was already seated. Her

ass tried to offer me a drink that she had sitting on the table, I be damned if I was about to drink that shit. Her trifling ass wasn't about to slip me no shit.

"Hey babe, what took you so long? I been waiting for about thirty minutes for you."

"Stop clocking my moves. I'm here now ain't I?"

"Damn what's wrong with you?"

"Nothing man, what you getting to eat?"

"I don't know, everything looks so good on this menu. Where did you hear about this place?"

"Don't worry about it, just eat up. Make it a good one."

Yo' ass better enjoy this last meal!

I sat there for over two hours trying my best to act like I wanted to be here for this fraud ass date. The more she talked about bullshit that I didn't give a fuck about, the more I was ready for this shit to be over with. I was so got damn uncomfortable.

When I check came I was fucking jumping on the inside. I paid that shit so got damn quick, I damn near broke my wrist trying to get my wallet out. We walked out, and it was time to get the next part of this plan going.

"So, am I going back to your place to chill? I need some good dick after that bomb ass meal." She said smiling and walking up on me. I hated when this bitch touched me.

"Yeah, we can do that. Aye, before we head to my joint, I need to drop off my car. My mans supposed to look at some shit on it for me.

"So, what you want me to do Len?"

Drop dead and muthafuckin die!

"Just follow me to the spot so I can drop the shit off." I headed to my car while she went to hers.

I sent Majik a text letting him know I was on my way, but not in so many words. We had damn near the whole police department in our pockets, but I still wasn't about to have shit tied back to me.

On the way to the warehouse, I rode in complete silence. I had so much shit on my mind I just needed a clear mind to think. For some reason, I was having second thoughts about getting rid of this hoe. I know it was something that had to be done though. She as the type of bitch that if scorned would make sure she snitched on your ass.

We pulled up, and I could already see her turning up her nose through my rearview mirror. Shit like this is what irritated me. Bitch stayed acting like she ain't just stop wearing mismatched colored bras and panties.

I got out and walked up to her car window. I had to make sure she wasn't on the phone or no shit like that before I tapped on her window. I didn't need her saying my name to no damn body.

"The hell you doing? Come on let me introduce you to my boy before we head out."

"Why we gotta do all that, why can't we just drop the car off and leave?"

"Got damn man, do you gotta complain about every fucking thing? Just come the fuck on."

I don't gotta be nice to this bitch anymore, and she was

starting to piss me the fuck off. Her stupid ass finally got out slamming the door and stomping behind me like a spoiled ass fucking child. I didn't give a damn about all that.

I walked in the door and made sure she was behind me. About two minutes of us being inside, Torrie was snatched from behind and dragged off to one of the side rooms. I could hear all the cussing and screaming she was doing. I had to quickly change my clothes, the sooner this shit was over, the sooner I could take my ass home.

When I made it to where she was at, she had calmed down due to the shit she was injected with. I didn't want her to be all the way knocked out. I needed her ass to be aware of why she was here and about to die.

I looked right into her eyes as I walked into the room.

"Lenyx what the fuck is going on?" she asked slurring her words.

"This is what happens when you can't shut the fuck up. You threaten my freedom, I take your life!" I told her as I screwed on the silencer on the gun.

"Wait, I would never snitch on youuuu." She was still trying to talk to me, but the drowsiness was taking over.

"I'll see you in hell bitch!"

There was no reason for me to go back and forth with her, it wasn't gonna change a damn thing.

I shot her twice in the chest and looked to my right and signaled these niggas to finish her ass off. They delivered about six or seven more shots, and just like that, her ass was good and dead.

Getting rid of her body, I did the shit without a care in the world and with the quickness. I let Majik know the shit was over with and lit me another J.

You ain't the one for me, baby
You ain't got shit I need, bitch
You want me to take my time with you
Well maybe I'm not your speed, bitch
Maybe I'm out your league, bitch
You ain't even got no cheese, bitch
Maybe I'm just too G for you
Or maybe I'm just too street, bitch
I can't even roll in peace (why)
Everybody notice me (yeah)

I rolled through the streets of Atlanta bobbing my head to that *Kodak Black Roll in Peace.* Listening to these lyrics, I couldn't do shit but laugh my damn ass off. This shit was everything that fit the muthafuckin moment. That bitch wasn't the one for me.

The next female that I gave my time to, I was gonna make sure she was the one. Until that time came though, these hoes can't get shit from me but this ten-inch dick in their guts. It was about to become bang a bitch season.

NAUTICA

*T*hings were getting weirder by the damn day. I was getting more and more threats as the days went by. I would be glad when either Draego found me, or Majik or them found his ass. I was sick and tired of looking over my shoulders and wondering if this going to be the day that he finds my ass.

I been waking up in cold sweats and shit thinking that nigga done found me. I have to say though, Majik has been a major help. When I wake up and can't sleep, I sometimes call him and sit and talk on the phone with him all night. He has never once complained about the amount of times I've cried during one of our conversations.

He has been hinting around a few times about me and him going out on a date, and I was curving his ass for the longest, but I think he done earned a date or two. I didn't want to have to deal with any fucking bullshit though from CoCo simple-minded ass. That bitch will make you catch a quick case.

Tonight was the night I finally gave in on this date shit. I don't know if I was really ready to be going out with a man, but I couldn't let Draego continue to fuck up my life. I know I needed to move on.

"What you got planned for the day bitch?" I asked Amaris walking in her room. The door was already open, so I didn't have to worry about knocking.

"Shit I wanted to stay in this fucking bed since it was my off day, but Jaysun's ass always wants to do some shit. Since Destiny isn't feeling too good, I'mma take Yanni over there to see her."

"Them two lil' heffas act like they can't stay away from each other."

"Girl, I had to bribe her ass just to go home last week. She was tryna stay over there all week, had her mama calling tryna go off on me."

I couldn't do nothing but laugh 'cause I already know how that shit went. Yanni was spoiled as fuck and Ahnais couldn't tell her lil' ass no for shit.

"I can imagine how that conversation went."

"What are you doing today? I hope your ass ain't planning on sitting in this damn house again!"

I've been hearing this same speech from them for weeks now. On my days off, all I do is sit around the house and scare myself to death. I was tired of just looking at these muthafuckin walls though.

"For your information bitch, I'm going out with Majik tonight."

I could see the look of disbelief on her face. She wasn't expecting me to say that. Everybody and their mama knows that his ass been tryna get me to go out with him for a minute now and I've done nothing but shoot him down, so I know this was a shock to her.

"Whaaaattttt, how the hell did that come about? Are you feeling ok?" her stupid ass asked me feeling my forehead.

I slapped her hand away from my head and playfully pushed her away from me. I had a smile on my face, and for the first time in a long while, I was actually happy and looking forward to something. I don't know if this will lead to something, but just the thought was giving me butterflies.

"Don't play with me girl, I'm feeling just damn fine. You already know we been talking day and night and I just finally decided to go ahead and accept his offer for a date, it's no big deal."

"Girl how in the hell are you gonna deal with CoCo and her bullshit? You know she stupid as fuck. I really don't wanna have to beat that hoe in her temple."

"I ain't worried about that dumb goat face ass cunt. That bitch comes my way with the bullshit and I'ma fuck around and cut her ass up and pour lemon juice all over her body. I ain't got time for that fuck shit."

"Hoe you going to got damn jail, you fucking maniac." Her ass was laughing like hell, but she knows it's some shit she would do.

I chilled with Amaris up until it was time for her to go spend time with her boyfriend. I really like him for her, so I wasn't even mad that we rarely got to spend time together.

After Maris left, I didn't really have anything to do to pass the time until my date tonight. I damn sure didn't want to continue sitting in this house. I decided to get up and go see Auntie Frankie, that way I could pass the time and get a few laughs in at the same time. It doesn't matter who you are, she was going to speak her mind and not have a care in the world while she was doing it.

I had already showered, so I grabbed a PINK outfit out the closet and threw it on with my UGGs, grabbed my shit and left. Walking to my car, I got that same everyday eerie feeling. Making it to my car as quick as I could, I always made sure to have my mace and knife in my hand when I was by myself.

I decided to call Majik because I still wasn't feeling right.

"What's up gorgeous?" just the sound of this nigga's voice had my ass all types of horny. This man shouldn't have this type of effect on me.

"Hey, are you busy? I was headed to Auntie Frankie's house, and I got that feeling again, I hate to bother you, and I can call you back if I'm disturbing you." I was so damn nervous talking to him and scared for my life all at the same time. I know I was rambling.

"Aye if you don't calm your ass down. Just keep driving to Frankie crib, ain't shit bout to happen to your ass. Know somebody always protecting you, so chill out. I'll be there waiting on you."

"Are you sure?" I asked looking around.

"So, you doubting me now? He asked sounding annoyed.

I wasn't trying to annoy him, I really wasn't. Nobody knew what it felt like though to know the man that beat your ass every day for literally nothing was after you and would probably kill you.

"No Majik, I'm not doubting you." I sighed heavily, I really wish he understood.

"I'll see you when you pull up shawty." He was back to his usual sounding self, so I guess he was over it.

I turned up the radio and blasted some of that old school R&B and continued on my way to my auntie house. I hoped she cooked something 'cause my ass was hungry as hell. My stomach was growling something serious. It didn't take me no time to get there, I was in a zone. I'm surprised I didn't get into a wreck.

When I pulled up, I saw Majik fine ass standing near his all-black Maserati. I don't think this man could ever have an off day. He made the simplest outfit look good. I got myself together before I got out the car.

Before I had gotten all the way out the car, he had already made his way to me.

"We gonna have to update your lil' car, it's cool and all, but you gonna have to match your man's fly."

"I'm just curious, who would my man be again?" I unintentionally smiled at him.

"Yo' ass better act like you know man, quit acting like you slow as fuck. You better be lucky a nigga like me was gracious enough to put you on my bus." He busted out laughing, even he knew that was some bullshit he was speaking.

"So, you Stevie J now? Are you slanging yo' beefcake all around Atlanta too? Oh wait, you might have a lil' Vienna sausage."

"Girl you got me fucked up, my dick ain't been that small since I was born. Shit, I done had a big dick since I been two years old."

I looked at this fool like he was crazy, only he would say some shit like that. The crazy thing about it, he said the shit with a straight face.

"Nigga, if you don't get the hell on talking stupid. I need to let my auntie know I'm here, you can continue this crazy ass conversation by your damn self."

I started up the steps and was almost to the door when Majik ran up behind me still talking shit. While he was in my ear with his foolishness, I made sure to ring the doorbell instead of just walking in. The last time I made the mistake of walking in her shit, she cussed my ass out for damn near three hours straight.

"I see you doubting me again, it's cool. Yo' ass gone learn one day to trust what ya man say."

"Whatever Mr. Majik, I'm not about to play with you today.

It took my auntie about two damn minutes to answer the damn door, and Majik stood there staring and smirking and me the whole time. I think he enjoys making me nervous. He knows his ass gets to me.

"Why the hell y'all retarded asses didn't just come in, the hell y'all ringing the damn bell for?"

I walked in and closed the door. I think my auntie starting to lose her mind or something.

"Auntie, didn't you just cuss me out the last time I came over here for just walking in your house? Are you getting early Alzheimer's? Just let me know, I'm here for you, help me help you?"

"Ain't shit wrong with my mind lil' ugly ass girl. I was mad that day, today, I'm having a good day."

"I promise I'mma get your mind looked at old lady."

"What the hell y'all doing together? You done finally gave him that snatch?"

"Shit, you'll know when I done had that pussy. When you see she walking funny, then you'll know she done had the Majik touch." He laughed, and I rolled my eyes.

"Anyway, what you been doing today Auntie?"

"Lil girl don't be trying avoid my got damn questions."

"She thought that bitch ass nigga was following her ass. Her ass was already on the way, I just met her ass over here."

"When y'all gonna handle that shit? I wish that punk ass nigga would bring his ass over this way. He gonna leave rolled up in rug and sent straight to hell."

It was never a dull moment with my auntie. Every time I spend time with her, it makes me miss my mother. I know if she were still alive, she would have killed Draego herself if she found out the shit he had done to me. After about an hour and a few laughs, Majik stood up to leave.

"Aye, I'm bout to head out. Come here and let me holla at you for a minute Nautica."

I stood up and followed him to the porch. He had a serious look on his face, so I was interested in knowing what the hell he had to say.

"What you call me out here for, what's up?"

"I'mma be by your joint to pick yo' ass up about eight tonight. Don't have yo' ass over here all day and not be ready when I come scoop you."

Shit, I thought he forgot about our lil' date or wasn't trying to go still. I guess I didn't get that lucky. It's not that I don't want to go, but I hate being around him alone. I'm not responsible for the shit that might happen. My ass ain't felt no dick in months, I'll fuck around seduce his ass.

"Where we going? I need to know what to wear."

"Man don't worry about all that, you ass know how to dress for a date. Don't you ass come out with a damn ballroom gown on, we ain't going to the fucking prom."

"Alright, I'll see you later."

"Remember what I said, ain't no need of you being scared, it's always somebody protecting your ass, and you'll never know it." he reminded me as he jogged down the steps and made his way to his car.

I hope his ass picked me up in that damn car. That shit was so pretty it was unreal.

When I made it back in there with auntie, her ass was trying to be damn nosey. This lady was something else. I'm mad I moved so far away and took so long to come back. I missed a lot of time with her and my damn cousins, but it's okay 'cause I plan to make all that time up. I'm here for good, and I know I won't ever let another man treat me like shit.

"Nauti, come here and sit down. Let me talk to you for a minute."

"Yes auntie, what's wrong?" I asked sitting next to her. I laid my head in her lap just to have feeling of being loved by a parent. This is something I know I'd do if my mommy was still here.

"I'm worried about you baby girl, you can't go through life afraid." I wasn't expecting for her to bring this up. She rubbed my hair and continued with her concerns. "You have to stop giving that clown ass nigga power over you. You're stronger than what you think you are. Boss the fuck up and act like the strong woman you were raised to be. You are gonna have to start living your life for you. I see Majik is feeling you and that's okay. He's a good man, but don't ever bring your old baggage on a new flight. You got me sunshine?"

"Yes ma'am, I got you. I understand."

"Good, now get on out of here and handle your business. I got shit to do later, I'm bout to turn out somebody's uncle or granddaddy." She said kissing my forehead and getting up laughing.

That's a vision that I could have really fucking did without.

I gave her a big ass hug and thanked her for that pep talk. I guess that's all I need, cuz I was feeling like superwoman. A bitch felt like she could for real take on the world. I didn't feel the need to look over my shoulders as I walked to my car or feel nervous about being out here alone.

That was just the talk I needed. I was about to reclaim my life. They thought I was a bad bitch before, they ain't seen nothing yet. Atlanta better get ready, Nautica is about to take over the Atl and it ain't a muthafucka out here that's gonna stop me.

MAJIK

I didn't wanna let Nautica know, but I was closer to finding this nigga than she thought. Of course, his ass wasn't still hanging around Chicago. I knew he was somewhere tryna find her and that's what we were banking on. She didn't know, but I have had somebody watching her since the day she told us about that fuck nigga. I was gonna make that nigga die a slow death. I didn't respect no nigga that beat on females. That was some bitch made shit.

I was at the warehouse with Lenyx's punk ass and Draiven counting up this money. I had a thing about using money machines, but these fools swore by it. I didn't trust shit but my fingers. Looking at the time I was glad I was bout done with this shit. I needed to get home so I could get dressed for this date. I've never in my damn life taken a woman out on a for real date. Me and CoCo use to grab a bite to eat every now and then, but I never consider the shit a fuckin date.

I put the band on the last stack of bills and handed them over.

"Aight punk ass niggas, I'm out this muthafucka. I got shit to do."

"Where yo' bitch ass going nigga?" Lenyx asked as he put the money in the duffel bag.

We weren't stupid by far, ain't no way we were leaving our money here. It was plenty of grimy ass niggas out here and would jump at the first chance to rob our asses if they could.

"Damn nigga you wanna hold my nuts too? Fuck you clocking my moves for?"

He shot me a bird and didn't bother going back and forth. I was glad 'cause I really didn't have time to be fucking around wit they ass. We'd sit around for hours just smoking and cracking jokes on each other.

"We need to link up first thing in the morning. I got word some niggas been tryna sell on our blocks out west." Draiven spoke up. That is the last thing I wanted to do. I planned on spending the whole day with my baby girl.

"Y'all might have to go scope out that shit without me, I'mma have baby girl tomorrow. If anything change I'll let y'all niggas know. You know how stupid her muthafuckin mama is"

"Aight nigga, I'm bout to bounce up outta here too. It's time to play hide the sausage wit Ahnais' ass."

"Man keep that bullshit to yo' self."

Grabbing my keys, I hurried up and got the fuck outta dodge. My ass was dippin in and out of that traffic, I'm surprised they didn't pull my ass the fuck over. I was going so damn fast I made it home in no time.

While pulling into my driveway, I instantly got annoyed. CoCo's stupid ass was sitting in her car waiting for me to get home. I can't imagine what the hell she was doing here, especially since Majesti was at my parent's crib. I open the garage and hurried up and pulled in that bitch and shut the door before she could even get out her car. I was not about to waste my time dealing with CoCo's stupid ass.

Making sure to put my alarm on before I headed upstairs, I could hear CoCo's ignorant ass still banging. I continued to ignore that shit as I sent Nautica a message telling her ass to make sure she was fucking ready on time.

I had to jump my ass in the shower and wash my damn balls. It wasn't nothing like some fresh nuts while out trying to impress a fine ass woman. I spent about thirty minutes doing what I needed to do and got out to get dressed.

Looking on my camera, I couldn't believe this bitch was still outside my house. You gotta be a special kind of stupid to sit outside somebody house when they don't want your ass there. I didn't have time to be worried about that goofy ass bitch though.

I threw on my dark blue Versace shirt with my medium colored jeans and my high top Giuseppe's. I sprayed on that good smelling Tom Ford cologne with a few of my jewels. I looked at myself in the mirror, and I had to admit, I was one fine ass dude with a big dick. I could see why I had bitches staking out my crib.

I turned off the lights turned on my alarm and jumped back in my car. As I pulled out the garage, CoCo got her Usain Bolt on and darted to the driver's side window banging on my shit like I won't beat the fuck outta her.

"Bitch you break my window and I'mma break your jaw." I rolled down my window and told her simple ass.

"This is the kind of shit you on Majik, you leave me outside like I'm some hoe ass trash!"

"Well technically you are, but that's beside the point. I don't recall inviting you to my spot, so I can't begin to understand why you are even here."

"I needed to talk to you."

"Look, man, I don't have time for this extra ass shit yo' ass, I got somewhere to be, so if you don't excuse me. You can get the fuck off my property."

"I promise you gonna regret the way you been treating me!"

"Now why you wanna go and threaten a nigga, you know I don't take to kindly to that shit."

I put my car in park and jumped out so damn quick, I don't think she saw it coming. I grabbed her face and squeezed the fuck out of her jaw, pulling her close to me I made sure she couldn't say she didn't hear what I had to say.

"That's yo' last time threatening me, you don't get no more chances wit me, bitch. All I asked you to do was chill the fuck out and take care of my daughter, but no you gotta be out here acting fucking stupid. Yo' hoe ass doesn't want for shit, and you still can't be satisfied. I got you though ma, you gonna feel me soon enough." Mushing her ass back, I jumped back in my car.

Of course she stood there with the crocodile tears, that shit didn't move me at all. I was over this shit wit my baby mama.

"Why are you still standing there Co?" she finally got the hint that wasn't shit bout to shake, and she carried her ass on to her car. Her dumb ass should have gotten that hint when she was left banging on my door.

Once she pulled out, I headed out right behind her. Now I was gonna have to dip and dodge this traffic to make it on time fucking around with that nonsense. I still had time to make it though, so I wasn't too worried. I went ahead and blazed up a fat ass blunt of some of the best shit. I needed to clear my damn head before I made it to Nautica.

I pulled up to Nautica house and checked my surroundings, stepping out I gave the nod to my security that only he would have seen. Knocking on the door, I could feel the shit Nautica was talking about, it felt like somebody was staring a hole right through my ass. I didn't do no amateur shit and look around, I just pulled out my phone and sent a text to Ralph. He was good at what he does, and that's why I trusted him fully with ole girl.

After about three minutes, she finally brought her ass to the door. I had to stop myself from acting like a simp ass nigga, cause shawty was for really looking right.

"Fuck took yo' ass so long to open the damn door?" that's the only thing I could think of to say.

This girl was so damn beautiful without even damn trying. Whoever her mama and daddy were, I wanna thank they asses.

"Well hello to you too, why are you always so damn rude?"

Even the way she frowned was cute as shit. I knew I was

gonna definitely gonna have to make this girl mine. She was working to have her own shit and wasn't a bitch just sitting on her ass waiting for somebody else to give shit to her.

"You look good as shit, you ready though?"

"Yeah, let me just grab my purse and phone."

She didn't need that shit while she was with me, but I let her do her thing, and we headed out. I had to ask Ahnais about this dating thing. I made some reservations and this fly ass restaurant downtown. I heard the room be spinning and shit overlooking Atlanta while you're eating shit. Seems like that would make a nigga dizzy, but whatever, niggas swore it was the shit, so we gonna see.

We were vibing like a muthafucka on the way to eat. The conversation flowed so naturally, it felt like I could talk to her all day. She was one of those people that when we talked, we could agree to disagree and we still understood one another. During all of our nightly conversations, that is one of the things that drew me to her.

During our date, I did all the shit I figured women like her would like. I fed her strawberries and shit, gave her plenty conversations and gave her my undividedundivided attention. I even pulled out chairs and opened doors for her. She better not ever say that my ass didn't try, I was doing shit all out of the norm for me.

After seeing Atlanta for at least three times, it was time for this shit to end. That shit went around slow as hell, and you couldn't even tell you were moving, but you knew. I was hoping she wouldn't mind spending some alone time with me at my crib.

A nigga wasn't trying to get no pussy for her ass, but I damn sure wouldn't turn it down if the shit just happened. I really wasn't ready to end my time with her.

"Aye, you wanna come to the crib and kick it wit a nigga?" wasn't no need in beating around the bust.

"What you think 'cause you fed me, now I'm supposed to give up the pussy?" she asked with a hint of attitude.

"First of all, calm your ass down. I get pussy thrown at me on a daily, so I damn sure don't have to pay for the shit. I was enjoying your company and didn't want the shit to end, but if you can't accept the fact that a nigga actually feeling yo' ass and ain't just trying to fuck, I'd be glad to take you back the fuck home."

I could tell I had embarrassed her but shit she had me fucked up. I really was feeling shawty, so I suggest she get that shit together.

"Look Majik, I'm sorry, and you're right, I shouldn't have assumed. I'm a bit paranoid about everything, and I shouldn't have taken my issues out on you. I'd like to continue our night if you don't mind."

Her looking at me with that sad ass face, it was hard to stay mad at her ass. I was gonna have to keep a pillowcase or some shit around if this shit with us with further. I needed to keep her face covered in order to stay mad at her.

"Yeah, whatever." Turning up the radio I didn't say shit else to her ass and headed towards my crib.

I must have been in a zone listening to that Makeveli cause we made it there in less than thirty minutes. A nigga wasn't really even mad, I just wanted to fuck with her for a lil' bit. I led her inside and in the living room while sending Ralph a text letting him off for the rest of the night.

"So, is this how you gonna act for the rest of the night? I apologize for my assumption, if you were gonna ignore me, why did you even bring me here?"

Taking off my hat, I rubbed my head. This damn girl was something else.

"I'm straight Nautica, chill out. Here's the remote to the TV, I'll be back."

I needed to get comfortable and get outta these damn clothes. I kept on my tank top and threw on my Nike short and Nike slides. By the time I made it back downstairs, her ass had done taken off her shoes and gotten comfortable. I lifted her feet off the couch and sat right next to her as I put them in my lap.

"You wanna watch a movie or some shit?" I asked while still rubbing her feet.

"Yeah, that's cool what you got good?

"Wait, we'd have to go upstairs in my room, I figured I'll tell you that before you say I'm trying to take advantage of yo' ass."

Laughing she threw a couch pillow at me and rolled her eyes.

"Come on stupid, don't be tryna get fresh and shit in the middle of the movie. I know I'm irresistible and all."

She chose *The Best Man Holiday* and snuggled up under me. If her ass didn't want me to drop this dick off up in her ass, she better move the fuck over. I started to rub my fingers in her hair, and before I knew, it dozed the fuck off.

~

 I woke up to the feeling of my dick being sucked, that shit was feeling so good a nigga thought he was dreaming. I opened my eyes to the prettiest site on this damn earth. Nautica ass was butt fucking naked looked good as fuck with her lips wrapped around my shit. Every time I tried to ask her what the hell she was doing, her ass made my damn toes curl. A nigga was straight up throwing up gang signs.

Her lips felt like a suction cup as she sucked my entire dick down her throat while playing with my balls.

"Oohhh shit girl, the fuck you doing?"

The amount of spit she had in her mouth while jacking my dick, and sucking all at the same time had a nigga ready to bust already. I ain't never in my life had a female suck my dick this good and make me bust this damn quick.

"Shit girl you about to make me nut."

It was all over when she did some damn trick with her tongue and her throat. I shot so hard down her throat my ass was seeing stars."

"Gahhhhhhhh damnnnnnnn, yoooo what the fuckkkk!"

I needed a minute, and her ass still had my dick in her mouth. I unintentionally push her back by her forehead.

"Nigga, the hell wrong with you?"

"Yo' ass gotta give me a second shit."

I looked over at the time and noticed it was damn near four in the morning. I hope she knows since her ass woke me up, she bout to give up that pussy.

After I took a few seconds to get myself together, I flipped her ass over and got on top of her. Kissing her like she was my girl, I used my fingers to play in that pussy. She was so damn wet already. My hand was damn near cover in her juices, I knew I was about to enjoy this.

"You sure you ready for this? Ain't no taking it back once it happens."

She shook her head, yes, and that's all I needed to know. Never in my life have I ever fucked somebody raw, but her ass was about to get it. My baby mama never even felt this dick without a rubber. The night she got pregnant she claimed the condom broke, but I still don't believe that shit.

Once I rubbed my dick up and down her pussy for a lil' bit, I put it in a lil' bit at a time. Her shit was so tight and warm, I put my head in the crook of her neck. Easing it in inch by inch, I was finally all the way inside, and I damn near wanted to marry this damn girl. I gave her a second to adjust to my size and started fucking the shit out of her ass. She made me nut quick as fuck the first time, so I had to show her what my ass really could do.

"Mmhhmmmm dammit Majik, I can't take this shit!"

I had her legs up in the crease of arms and once I found that G-spot, it was no way I was bout to let up.

"Nah take this shit, you wanted the Majik so yo' ass got i-" I couldn't even finish the damn sentence her pussy was feeling so damn good "damn girl what the fuck you got in this shit?"

Ain't no way in hell she was leaving here without being my damn girl. Her ass can't be giving a nigga pussy this good and think I wasn't getting this shit again. I see why that bitch ass nigga was stalking her ass. Shit after feeling this shit, I was bout ready to put a GPS tracker on this pussy.

She was bout to have me going out like a sucker, so before my ass nutted to damn soon, I pulled out and ate the hell out of her pussy. She even had me eating ass, and a nigga hasn't ever been a salad tosser. Once I made her cum, I went right back to fucking the shit out of her. After damn near fucking for over an hour in every position possible, I finally busted a big ass nut on her soft,

Falling straight down on top of her, I was breathing hard as fuck. I swear I think this girl just put some got damn voodoo on me. I'mma start calling her ass Sunshine like the bitch on the movie *Harlem Nights*.

I hurried up and went to the bathroom to get us a washcloth to wipe us down. By the time I made it back in the room her ass was knocked out. I cleaned us both off and jumped back onon the bed, put the covers back on us, pulled her to me and took my ass right back to fucking sleep.

AMARIS

I had been splitting my time between work and spending time with Jaysun and Destiny. My ass was worn the fuck out, but I'd never tell his ass that. He'd been spending less time in the streets and more at home with Des. I could tell her health was starting to decline more and more as the days went by. I did everything I could to try and keep her happy and smiling. It seemed like all she wanted was Yanni over, but she never had the energy to play once she came. They would just lie in her bed and read books and watch TV.

It was almost that time for me to clock out and I was gonna run to that damn time clock so fucking fast. I couldn't wait to get home and take me a long ass nap. I could hear my bed calling me now. Once I got done giving my reports to the night nurse, I got the hell outta dodge.

I didn't even give a damn about turning on the radio as I

drove through the streets of Atlanta. A few minutes into my drive I was getting text messages back to back, and then a call from Jaysun came through.

"Hey babe, what's going on?" I answered

"Man, its bad. She ain't breathing, I can't lose my baby girl man, I just can't lose her." He said, but I could barely understand what he was saying because he was crying so damn hard.

"Calm down Jaysun, where are you at now?"

"Children's Hospital of Atlanta, the one she was at the last time."

"I'm on the way, I'll be there in a few minutes. I'm not too far."

Aight was all he said before he hung up on me. I wasn't gonna take that shit personal cause I couldn't imagine what he was going through. I sent up a quick prayer as I made my way inside to find him.

The waiting room was jam-packed with everybody. My sister, Yanni, and even the fellas was there. I wonder how long she has been here for all them to be here. The first person I went to was Jaysun, I'd talk to everyone else afterward.

"Hey baby, what are they saying?" I asked him as I sat with him and his mama.

"We're still waiting for the doctor to come out and update us." His mom answered for him.

He sat on the edge of his seat with his head in his hands with the tears constantly rolling down his face. I wish there was something I could do to make all this better. I rubbed his back with my head laying on his shoulder.

The room was so quiet you could hear a pin drop. Three hours later the doctor finally came out, and the look on his face wasn't a good one. We all stood and crowed around to hear what he had to say.

"Destiny stopped breathing, and we were able to resuscitate her back, but her heart wasn't strong enough. The cancer spread throughout her body and heart just couldn't take it. I'm sorry Mr. Williams, she didn't make it, and we tried everything."

"So, you tryna tell me my daughter is gone, is that what you're saying doc? Nah that can't be what the fuck you saying. Man, fuck that go try again, she wouldn't just leave me" he broke down as he grabbed the doctor "Doc please you gotta go try, I can't live without my baby, please go try again."

Me and his mama did everything we could to try to get him to let the doctor go, but he wasn't budging.

"Nooooooooo go get my best friend, you didn't try hard enough. She wanted me to come spend the night tonight, so I know she wasn't ready! Go get her NOWWWWWW!" even Yanni started hitting him with her little fist.

The whole room felt the loss of Destiny, there wasn't a dry eye in the room. Draiven had to restrain Yanni with his whole body because she just wouldn't calm down.

"Again, I'm sorry, Nurse Tasha will take you to see her if you wish," The doctor said walking away with a look of sorrow.

"Fuck your sorry, your sorry won't bring my baby back." He said as he picked up a chair and threw it and slid down the wall to the floor.

"I'm so sorry baby, come on let's go and see her." I suggested

"The fuck you mean go see her, these muthafuckas better bring my baby back."

I wasn't gonna take offense to the way he was talking to me because I knew he was hurting. I looked to his mama for some help even though I knew she was really in pain too. She quickly put her feelings to the side to talk some sense into Jaysun, which took a while but he finally listened.

I didn't want to overstep my boundaries, so I just let him and his mother go in first, and I would go in with Yanni. I didn't know how she was gonna handle this so I was really debated on whether or not we should let her do this. After giving it a thought, I figured the best thing to do would be to just talk to her.

"Yanni come here, let TeTe talk to you" She was still crying and was hurting bad "do you think you can handle going back there or do you want to just go home?" I asked rubbing her hair.

"I wa wa wanna go back thereee." She struggled to get out.

I wasn't convinced, but I had to take her word for it. As long as her mama was cool with it, I guess I had to be also.

Jaysun was back there so long, I was tempted to go check up on him. Not long after the thought crossed my mind, I saw him coming from the back. I gave him another hug and told him I'd be right back.

The walk to the room felt like it was long as shit, but it really wasn't. Ahnais went and kissed her on the forehead and stepped back to allow us a minute to have our moment.

"I'mma miss you, pretty girl. I wish I could have had longer with you, I'm thankful for the time I got to spend with you. Rest well, angel." I rubbed her head and gave her a kiss.

Ayanni took a slow walk towards the bed and just stood there staring at Destiny. Before anyone could stop her, she ran and jumped on the bed.

"Wake up Destiny, wake up, we have to play. I promise I won't be bad or fight anymore, just wake up" she proceeded to shake her, and the shit broke my damn heart. This was the only person she had ever connected with. They'd been connected at the hip for months. I guess Jaysun heard the commotion because he came busting in the room "Mr. Jaysun, help me wake her up, she's isn't ready to go. I have to spend the night tonight remember."

He stood there crying for a few seconds as we continued trying to pry her from the bed. He moved us aside and told us to let him handle it.

"Baby girl, we have to let her go. Trust me I don't want to, but we have to." He said picking her up from the bed.

"But why?" she asked still crying laying her head on his shoulder.

"Cause God needed her more than we did. You don't want her here in pain, do you?"

"No, but I would have made her feel better. She like when I beat people up for her. I could have just beat up somebody."

The whole room busted out laughing in the middle of us crying our eyes out.

"I know baby girl, but she's up there in no more pain. The good thing about it is she'll always be with us right here." He pointed to her chest.

I guess that was good enough for her cause she calmed down and walked back over to the bed.

"I'll let you sleep Desi, but that don't mean I have to like it." she kissed her and walked out.

I don't know how we are gonna get through this, this shit was gonna be hard. We all left out to let them get her ready to go to the funeral home. The next few days were gonna be rough as hell.

AHNAIS

hings haven't been the same with Yanni ever since
Destiny passed. She has been withdrawn and barely
wants to talk to anybody. Right after the funeral her dad offered
to take her anywhere she wanted to go, and she declined. It's
been months, and it's time to figure something out cause this
isn't the Yanni I used to. She didn't even want to go to my
mom's house, and you normally couldn't keep her ass from
over there.

Draiven had plans to try and get her mind off the situation.
He invited the whole family out to Dave & Buster, he knew her
tomboy ass would like that shit. I was already up dressed and
ready, and it was time to get her up.

When I walked into the room, she was looking at a picture of
her and Destiny that was taken just before she died.

"Hey, my baby, how long you been up?"

She shrugged her shoulders and laid back down.

"Get up and get dressed, we got things to do today."

"For what, why do I have to be involved?" she said with an attitude.

I understand she was taking this hard, but she was two seconds from getting her ass knocked clean off her shoulders. She must have forgotten who she was talking to. I was about to quickly remind her ass.

"Ayanni, don't play with me, get your ass up and do what I said, and you got an hour to be ready. You better watch who the hell you talking to lil girl."

I guess Draiven heard me getting loud so of course, he comes in after the fact as if I need his help. Yanni finally got up to start doing what I told her to do when I noticed the tears rolling. It was hard to stay mad at her, but I still was ready to knock her teeth loose.

"Go head Ahnais, I got her." Of course, he wanted to step in and be super dad.

Where the fuck was he at when she was giving me all that fucking attitude. They both had me fucked up. I didn't even reply, I rolled my eyes and walked out.

I didn't have shit to do since I was already dressed, so I just went down to the living room to watch some TV and wait for their asses. It wasn't long before I heard someone come down the stairs.

"Yo what the fuck was that shit Nias?" I know this stupid ass nigga must have bumped his dead head or some shit.

"What the fuck you mean, her ass was losing her mind, so I was helping her find it."

"You act like you don't know what our daughter is dealing with. Did you really have to do all that?"

"Look I don't know why I am standing here explaining my actions, but just because she is going through something it doesn't give her the right to talk to me like she done lost her fucking mind."

"I'm not saying that Ahnais, all I'm getting at is that you could cut her a little break. We have never had a problem with her, so it's obvious that she is still feeling a way about her friend."

"Whatever Draiven, you got it. Let me know when it's time to go, I'll be in my room."

This shit that's going on with my child and that blackmailing ass bitch Tatiana was about to drive me crazy. He was still getting text messages from that dumb bitch, and I was seconds off that ass. The way she was carrying on, one would think they really had something going on, it's a good thing I knew my nigga 'cause his ass wasn't that got damn stupid.

I couldn't wait until they got to the bottom of the shit and found out what the hell was going on. I wanted to know like hell who could have beef with them. It felt like we had bullshit coming at us from every fucking angle.

It didn't take long for them to do what they needed to do cause before I knew it, Draiven was letting me know it was time to go. We loaded up and headed to try and have some fun. While in the car, I tried to engage in a conversation with Yanni, but she didn't say much and put her headphones on the majority of the ride. It's ok because I was hoping this outing would put a smile on her face.

We pulled in, and everyone was in the parking lot waiting for us. Once we got out, and she noticed Amaris and Jaysun first and took off running toward them. I wish I had that effect on her, but anything or anyone that made her open up and happy, I was okay with.

"What are you doing here TeTe?" Yanni asked with a smile on her face.

"I came to spend time with my favorite girl if that's okay with you missy."

"I guess we can go on back home then Amaris, Yanni don't want us here?" Jaysun playfully pulled my sister like he was getting ready to leave. I was happy to see he was doing okay considering it was his daughter that passed.

"No uncle Jaysun, I have to beat you in this basketball game. My daddy can't play at all and mama is too much of a girl."

"Excuse you, young lady, don't hate cause your mama is fly as hell." She laughed, and that was the first real interaction I have had with her in a minute. I am starting to think this was a good ass idea.

"So yo lil' big head ass don't see me standing here? Shit, I can take my ass the fuck home hell, I got shit I could be doing. Got me out here with this ugly got damn lil' girl and she can't even speak. Who the fuck raised her lil' rude ass?"

Everyone busted out laughing at my mama because she was actually serious, she was mad as hell.

"NaNa, why are you so extra, you didn't even give me a chance to speak," Yanni said as she went over trying to hug her. My mama wouldn't allow her to as she mushed her head away from her.

"Nah, get the fuck away from me. Don't come over here now trying to hug me and shit. Come the fuck on in here so we can get this shit over with."

"Mama, how old do NaNa have to be before we can put her in a home?" Yanni tried to whisper to me, but unfortunately for her, my mama heard her.

"Lil girl I just bout smacked the shit out of you just then!"

Yanni ran over to her daddy cause she knew my mama would have really smacked her ass, she don't care about being out in public. She will act out no matter where she at. When we made it in and found a section big enough for all of us, it didn't take no time for everyone to start enjoying themselves. It was good to see my baby girl enjoying herself for the first time in a while, Jaysun even seemed to be having a good time. We spent so much damn money in that place, jumping from game to game. The time had gone by so fast, we had been in there for hours. I was damn near drained, but I knew this day was nowhere near over. We had so much shit planned, I was probably gonna need a hot bath and some Epsom salt by the end of the night.

We were all sitting down grabbing a quick bite to eat when I saw a familiar face walking towards our table. Before I had a chance to get Draiven's attention, this bitch had the audacity to come up to us like she was a part of our circle. She just don't know I would be the hell out of her without a second thought.

"Well, well, well, hello there Draiven?"

"Yo Tatiana, on some real shit, don't bring no bullshit over here. We tryna enjoy our day, so get the fuck on now for real."

"Damn, it's like that? I was just coming over here to speak to my future family." This bitch really said that shit with a smirk on her face.

She must really don't know that I will beat her ass without a second thought.

"You must be tryna get your ass beat today?" I asked her as I started to stand up when Draiven pushed me back down.

"Damn girl, why you so violent? I just wanted to come see how our nigga was doing?"

"Girl you ain't nobody to my daddy. Mama can we slap her, please? She aggravating my soul and you know I don't like to be aggravated."

I know Yanni was getting back to herself cause she was talking reckless. I was wrong for not immediately getting on to her for the way she was speaking to an adult, but the shit was funny as hell.

Things were more than likely about to go from bad to worse. I saw the look in Majik's eyes, and it wasn't a good one. Him and Nauti have been kicking it tough, so I was praying she would be able to stop what was about to happen.

"Bitch, I will splatter your brains all over this muthafuckin table and go home and sleep peacefully. Get the fuck on before you piss me off." Majik told her as he started to reach for his gun.

"It's about time uncle Majik, just shoot her so we can eat."

"Yanni, shut your grown ass the fuck up."

"You pull out a gun in front of me but then get mad. How smart is that uncle? I just want to eat though."

"SHUT UP YANNI!" everyone yelled at the same time. She shrugged her shoulders and continued to eat her food.

Tatiana got some sense about herself and went on about her business. I couldn't wait until she got what the fuck was coming to her. It was pissing me off that Draiven's stupid ass wouldn't let me beat the fuck out of her just one good damn time. That bitch was trying to make me look like I was weak as fuck.

I heard about her going around telling people that she fucked my nigga. It's aight though cause he didn't have but another hot minute to get this shit under control.

It didn't take long for things to go back to normal once that skank bitch left. We continued enjoying ourselves and moved on to the next phase of our day.

DRAIVEN

I've been slipping with handling my business while making sure shit at home was taken care of. Now that my baby girl was pretty much back to her normal self, I could focus more on finding out who the hell was coming after us. I know Majik had been on it, but we weren't really coming up with anything. There were a few names being tossed around, but nothing too concrete.

I was headed to holla at my nigga Kwame, and I hope like hell he had something for me. It was at the point that I didn't give a damn who was behind this shit, I was bout to end that lil' bitch Tatiana's life. She was taking me for a joke, and a nigga wasn't beat for this shit. All it would take is for one lil' punk ass nigga to get wind of the fact that we was slacking for them to come and try us up.

I wanted to get all this shit out the way cause I was ready to make an honest woman out of Ahnais and I couldn't do that with all this extra nonsense lingering. I be damned if I let another man snatch her up.

Once I pulled up to the hood, I grabbed my gun and my sack of that good loud and locked up my car. I made sure to put the alarm on cause niggas round here didn't care bout who they stole from. I got stopped by a few dope heads like I was a corner boy ass nigga and a few hood hoes looking for a come up.

Knocking on Kwame's door, I was getting irritated cause it was taking him so fucking long to come to open it up. That shit was putting me on edge.

"What the fuck took yo ass so long to open up? A nigga like me don't trust shit like that, I'mma think you tryna set me the fuck up or something." I told Kwame' as I walked up in his place looking around.

"As much work I done put into tryna figure who the hell coming after y'all, I wouldn't have had time to set you the hell up nigga."

"Shit, I hope you got something for me then, I'm ready to get this shit handled and put behind me."

"Man, I had to go through hell to find just the smallest thing. After digging for a while, I came across the names Roman and Soloman Baressi, do those names ring a bell?"

"Hell nah, am I supposed to know who that is?"

I was racking my brain tryna remember if I had heard those names before, but nothing was coming to my mind.

"All I could gather was it was some Italian brothers who got it out for you, Majik, and Len. They been tryna get at y'all niggas for the last year or so. I got a few people looking deeper into their background, I was able to get pictures of what they look like."

Kwame' handed me a thick folder of information he had on the Baressi brothers, and I was even more confused than I was before I got here. We've never had business with the Italians, so I had no idea what they could want with us.

I wasn't about to let this take up too much of my time, we would have to handle it whenever it came our way.

Tatiana didn't have no more time to play with me though, she wanted to enter and play in a grown man's game, I was gonna show her how this shit is really done. She done let some mutha-fuckas I didn't even know cause her to lose her life. I was killing her and anybody that wanted to jump in to try and save her. I'd already had a lil' bit of info on her ass and knew where she laid her head at.

We kept her working for us just so that we could keep eyes on her, I even moved her to one of the warehouses that we didn't do much in. It took us a minute to move shit around cause I don't know what info her scandalous ass done gave out and we worked too hard to have our shit come crumbling down.

I had to hit up the fellas and let them know that we needed to meet up in a few hours. I couldn't let them walk around with a known enemy targeting us and I not let them know about it. After I gave Kwame' a few more things to handle for me, I raised up out of there. I had more important shit to get done, and I needed to hurry up and make it on time.

Jumping back in the car, I had twenty minutes to make it to my next destination. I sped through the streets and swerving from lane to lane, there was no way in hell I was bout to be late. I made it there with a few minutes to spare, so I took a few seconds to get myself together and clear my mind.

My chest was beating fast as hell as I walked into the jewelry store. I know I was making the right choice but shit, a nigga, was sweating like hell. I had my future mother in law, Amaris, and Nautica meet me here to help me pick out the best ring for Ahnais.

"Boy bring your ass on in here, the hell you dragging your feet for? You should have been did this shit? Mama Frankie found any reason to show her ass. I should have known she was gonna talk shit though, it wouldn't be her if she didn't.

"Keep on talking shit old lady, I'mma make sure your ass get put in a nursing home when you get old" joking around with them put me at ease, I guess it's just what I needed.

This was a fancy ass jewelry store, they was serving wine, fruit, and all kinds of shit. I ain't never seen no shit like that. I done been in Zale's plenty of time and they never gave my ass no damn fruit.

"Good afternoon sir, my name is Tiffany, and I'll be the jeweler assisting you. Is there anything specific you are looking for today?" this bitch was standing there trying to give the come fuck me look. I know got damn well she see me here with all these damn women. I was about to check her ass, but Nautica's crazy ass beat me to it. I'm starting to think every woman in this family crazy as hell.

"Look hoe, his ugly ass is already spoken for, so I suggest you stop trying to suck dick on the job and show us the engagement rings."

I could tell Nautica embarrassed the hell out of her cause her face was all red and flustered. She was gonna get put in her place, but I was gonna be a little bit nicer. Shawty didn't look me in the eye at all, and when she had a question, she directed it to one of the women first. I didn't feel bad for her ass though, these hoes needed to have some kinda respect for themselves.

After spending two hours and looking at over thirty rings, I was getting frustrated as hell. It shouldn't be this hard to find a damn ring. I was seconds from going to find that twenty-five dollar ring that was going around the internet. This shit wasn't about to drive me damn crazy. I damn near gave up when I looked up and saw the ring I knew was made just for my girl. It was a princess cut with one and a half carats, white gold halo with round pave diamonds down the sides.

"Oh my damn, Draiven, this is it, this is the oneeeee!" Amaris squealed out, jumping up and down with Nautica like a teenage damn school girl.

"I swear if y'all don't shut the fuck up, I'm shooting both of y'all in the fucking knees." They immediately stopped jumping up and down and gave me the death stare. It looked like these broads was about to try and jump me.

"Don't get cute in front of these uppity ass folks Draiven, I will still smack the shit out of you, don't threaten my baby. Get this damn ring and come on, I got shit to do."

"Ma can I ask you something, like real shit. Since the first day I met you, you been hollering you got shit to do, like what the hell you gotta do fam?

"I gotta go fuck yo daddy, now pay for this shit and come the hell on"

Standing there. I couldn't do shit but laugh. Looking at the ring one more time, I battled with myself back and forth on if I should have gotten it custom made.

"Aye y'all sure this the one"

"DRAIVEN!" they all yelled at the same time

"Aight damn" they can't blame a nigga for wanting this shit perfect. I pulled out my black card and handed it to lil' Ms. Jewelry lady.

I caught the look in her eyes when I gave her my card. She looked like she was again ready to pop that pussy on a hand-stand. This is exactly why I didn't care about becoming a one-woman man for life. It's too many money hungry bitches out here for me.

After ringing me up, this broad went to box it up in the back and was taking her time. Once she came back with the ring, she gave it to me and handed me my receipt along with another piece of paper. Looking at it I noticed it was her number and she had the nerve to wink at me.

This is why niggas treat these hoes like they ain't shit. I

clearly got a girl and this trash bag hoe still throwing herself at me. I waved Nautica and Amaris over so they could see this bullshit. I didn't even say nothing, I just handed it over. Their faces immediately scrunched up, and I knew they was bout to turn up in this place. Leaning on the display counter, my ignorant ass got ready for the show.

Before Ms. Jewelry lady knew what was coming, Amaris reached up and slapped her so fucking hard spit flew out her mouth and landed on my shirt. Nautica followed it up with two quick hits to her jaw.

"Got damn man, the fuck y'all do that for?"

"Do what, I know you ain't taking up for this off-brand bitch"

"Why the hell you get that bitch spit on my muthafuckin shirt. That's so got damn unsanitary man."

Once I saw who I guess was the manager come from the back, I had a feeling I was gonna have to show my ass.

"Excuse me what is going on here? We do not allow this kind of behavior here."

"Fuck you and this store. You need to teach your hoe ass employees how to do their job without trying to hop on dicks" Frankie had her hand on her hip and said. Just waiting for him to say something stupid back to her, she stood there ready and willing to act a fool.

"I'm going to have to ask you all to leave before I'm forced to call the police."

"Dude, fuck you and the police. I bet I won't buy shit else from this muthafucka" I threw the piece of paper with ole girl's number on it at the middle of that short, fat, pudgy, white mutha-fucka's head.

He turned beet red he was so mad. Let me get the hell up outta here before I end up locked up playing around. I calmed the girls and ma Frankie down and got the hell up out of there, and after I made sure they got to their cars safe, I got the hell on.

COCO

J never thought it'd come a time where I wouldn't have Majik. I knew he was getting tired of me, but I thought I would be able to get him to overlook the shit like I had been doing for years. Being with a man like him was like a dream come true. I came from nothing, eating for real struggle sandwiches. When I got with Majik my life went from shit to sugar, and I wasn't ready to leave the life I was accustomed to. Things were all good with us until that dumb bitch Nautica came along. I even went as far as trying to get pregnant again, knowing damn well I didn't want any more kids, I barely wanted the one I got. I dropped Majesti's smart mouth ass off every chance that I got, but I felt like if I got pregnant again, it would be enough to make him wanna work it out. If he damn thinks I was gonna just sit back and let him build something with another bitch, he had life fucked up.

While I figured out what I needed to do to repair my family, I was bout to get out here in these streets and do me. I wasn't an ugly bitch by no means, and I've always had men tryna holla at me. Standing five feet three inches, I was about two shades darker than a paper bag. I had flawless skin with a banging ass body and could pull a man just by the blink of my eye. I couldn't and wouldn't accept just anybody though, I wanted a man that could afford to support me.

I was planning on hitting up the club tonight to see who I could bag and snag but didn't see shit in my closet I would have wanted to wear. My thoughts were interrupted by the ringing of my phone. Looking at the screen, I saw it was my best friend, Kaycie. She's just the person I needed to talk to, her ass was always ready to turn up somewhere.

"What's the tea hoe" I plopped down on my bed and answered.

"Bihhhh, why I saw your baby daddy out last night at wit his lil' hoe at Pappadeaux."

"Fuck Majik and bitch what your broke ass doing at Pappadeaux?"

"Shiiit you must be tweaking and geaking, as long as I got a good working pussy, I'll never be broke."

"I know that shit's real bestie. I need to get out tonight and find Majesti a stepdaddy, you tryna kick it tonight?" I asked cleaning under my fingernails with a nail file. I looked hard at my nails and added a manicure on the list of shit I needed to do.

"You know you didn't even need to ask, hell yeah I'm down. That nigga Zane starting to bore me, it's time to get a replacement for his ass." she laughed in my ear loud as hell, popping gum continuously back to back wit her ghetto fabulous ass.

"Aight, well I need to go grab me something from the mall to wear. I'mma send Maj over there wit her people."

"Shit, you might as well come by and scoop me up."

"Bet, I'll be there in bout thirty minutes, so you better be ready. If you not, I promise I'mma leave you."

Once I hung up with Kaycie, I sent a text to Majesti's Nana to see if I could drop off until tomorrow. She told me I had to wait a few hours, so I didn't have a choice but to take her with me for now. You better believe just as soon as she was home, I was gonna be right there knocking like I'm the Jehovah Witness.

It wasn't that I didn't love my child because I did, I just didn't know how to be a mama. I never really had one to show me. The only reason why I even kept her was because Majik found out before I could go have an abortion. I was glad he wanted her at first because I thought that would keep him in my life, but as you can see that shit was a no go. He was a good ass father though but wasn't shit shaking for me. My mama ain't never do shit for me but beat my ass whenever she got drunk. I don't even know why her ass didn't go to the nearest clinic when she had me. Don't get me started on my daddy or my sperm donor cause that nigga wasn't shit either. I probably passed his assed on the street somewhere and never knew it. Last I heard, he was somewhere on crack real hard. I don't feel sorry for his ass, not one bit, that's what the fuck he gets for having a child and not taking care of it. Fuck him and my bum ass mama.

I pulled up to the mall with Kaycie and was ready to tear shit up. Majik hadn't completely cut off my access to the account he had for me, and I was grateful. I was bout to pop some tag

We went from store to store just grabbing all kinds of shit, things I'd never probably wear, but I got it anyway.

"Ma I'm tired, and I'm hungry," Majesti complained with an attitude. This is exactly why I didn't wanna bring her lil' ass.

"Lil girl if you don't shut yo ass up."

"Tuh, and watch me tell my daddy" she immediately took her phone out and started texting before I could grab it.

It wasn't even two minutes later when my phone rung. I started not to answer it, but I knew it would just make it worse. I wish like hell he never got her that damn phone. She does this all the fucking time.

"Yes, Majik!" I rolled my eyes and answered.

"Yo why the fuck are you threatening my muthafuckin child bitch? If she hungry stop what the fuck you doing and feed her. Keep on with the dumb shit and you better not say shit to her."

"Anything else sir Majik."

"Yeah, get the fuck off my line." Yeah, his rude ass hung up on me.

I looked at Majesti, and she had an I dare you look on her face. I don't know why I didn't swallow her ass. I got the last thing I needed in this store, and we headed to the food court. Of course, my spoiled fucking child had to choose what we ate like it was only one restaurant here.

I wasn't gonna let my Majik and his demon spawn twin get under my skin. I found the perfect outfit for tonight, so I was too hype. Looking over to my right, I thought I saw a familiar face.

Majesti saw it too because just as quick as I blinked my eye, she took off running.

"Ain't that your daughter's step mama, " laughing with a mouth full of food, Kaycie thought she was real funny. I wanted to hit her in her throat and make her fucking choke.

Kaycie was one of those bitches you kept around you cause you know she could never outshine you. I swear sometimes I wanted to smack the shit out of her. She always thought the wrong shit was funny.

Looking over I watched how my child clung to her, and it pissed me off. They looked like the perfect mother-daughter duo. Yeah, this hoe had me all the way bent. It was time to put a stop to this.

This shit is about to be very interesting.

I started walking towards her table with nothing but being petty on my mind. She wants to be with Majik, well get ready to meet the baby mama from hell.

NAUTICA

I heard someone calling my name, and when I looked up, I saw my honey bun running towards me. Majesti was my baby, and no one could tell me any different.

I'd been dealing with Majik pretty heavy for the last few months so of course, I was going to have a relationship with his daughter. People always talked about how bad Majesti was, but she never acted that way with me.

"Nautiiiiii."

"Hey honey bun, what you doing here? Who are you with?" I asked looking around. I spotted her stupid, bitter ass mama walking towards our table and instantly started praying that I didn't have to lay her the hell out.

Ever since Majik stop fucking with her for real, she been on some real bitter bullshit. She even tried to stop him from seeing

Majesti, but that didn't last long when she realized she wouldn't have a babysitter to go club hopping.

"My mother," she rolled her eyes, and if she rolled them any harder, they'd be stuck "why you didn't come get me so I could have come with you?"

"I'm sorry baby girl, we will do something tomorrow."

"Ohhh can we go to th-" she didn't get to finish what she was bout to say cause her ignorant ass mama came over here with the bullshit.

"Did I tell your ass you could get up and run off," she tried pulling her by the arm, but I wasn't bout to have that.

"I wanted to come see Nautica, and I did," she was rolling her neck with her hand on her hip.

"Umm no honey bun we don't disrespect adults, we talked about that remember."

"I'm sorry Nauti, can we still go somewhere tomorrow?"

"Yes, but only if you are being good."

"Umm, I don't need your ass tryna tell my daughter what the fuck to do. You aren't her mother, I think I fucked Majik and had her"

"Watch your tone CoCo, you know I'm wit it all day." Ahnais didn't even bother looking up from her food as she put CoCo's scary ass in her place.

"I'm saying tho, why is your cousin tryna play mother with my daughter."

"Majesti go over there and finish your food, I'll see you tonight" she gave me a big hug and did as she was told.

I waited until she was seated and out of earshot before I cursed her mama out.

"First, ain't nobody tryna play mother to your child, but maybe if you spent half the time with her as you did in the streets or chasing my nigga, you wouldn't feel so threatened."

"Bitch, you just a fill-in until Majik come back to his family" she was tryna get loud.

"You done been warned once about your tone, don't get slapped."

"CoCo, you already know how I'm coming. You done been saved a few times from me beating yo ass. Keep fucking with my family, and it won't be a nigga on this earth that will be able to stop me."

"Nah I got it cuz," I didn't need CoCo thinking I needed somebody to fight my battles. "Whether me and Majik last ain't got shit to do with how you were just talking to Majesti. You need to be more concerned about her instead of trying to sit on her daddy's dick and spend his money."

"Y'all not about to be tryna double team her."

"Kaycie, girl shut yo ass up, you know you can't fight." I swear Ahnais stupid for that one. I couldn't do shit but laugh.

I wasn't about to continue going back and forth about nothing in the middle of the food court. We threw our food away and left CoCo standing her stupid ass right there looking stupid. I continued doing what I came to do. This was my first day off in the last nine days, and I'm gonna take full advantage of it.

Being at the hospital daily and seeing how much of a difference people in the healthcare make, I was seriously thinking about furthering my education and doing something different. I wanted to work in the lab, so I needed to look into that.

We went to Victoria's Secret, so I could take advantage of their sale they had going on. Everything in sight that I saw, I grabbed it up. I finished doing what I needed to do and carried on with the rest of my day.

*T*he next day...
    I didn't get to see Majik yesterday because he had to spend time with his daughter and handle shit in the streets. She called me over and over wanting me to come see her, but I felt like they needed time together without me. I promised I'd see her today though and I planned on keeping that promise.

I had been out and about looking at apartments all morning, and I was getting frustrated. I didn't come across nothing that I felt was right for me. I hadn't told anyone I was trying to move out cause I didn't wanna hear their mouths about it. I've still been getting crazy messages, phone calls, and other bullshit that I couldn't explain, but I wasn't about to let Draego control my life. I needed to give Amaris her space back. She's barely there, but it was just the principle.

I put the apartment hunting on the back burner and made my way to the school I was looking to apply at. I had a degree in Business but that wasn't what I really wanted to do. My plan was to go back to school years ago, but of course Draego wasn't having that. Now, there wasn't nothing or nobody here to stop me and I was glad about that.

I signed up for financial aid and spoke to my assigned counselor to discuss what classes I would need to take. Once I was done, I took my time just walking around checking out everything. I ended up in the cafeteria and looking around, and I could have sworn I saw a blast from my past. It was so many people in my way that before I could get a better look the person was gone.

I just said I wasn't gonna let Draego control my life, but just that quick the thought of him being possibly this close to me had me shaking. Sitting down at the nearest bench and called Majik. I hated having to call him every time I broke down about this bullshit.

"Where yo ass at? You got Majesti getting on my nerves man."

"Majik I think he's here. I saw him, I know I saw him!"

"What I tell you about letting another nigga that ain't me get you worked up and in yo feelings?"

"I know but what if he gets to me."

"Nautica I ain't gonna say the shit again, chill out and bring your ass on over here."

"Are you listening to anything I'm saying?"

"We not about to go back down this road again are we? I asked you if you trusted me with your life and you told me yes."

"I do trust you."

"So why are we even having this discussion then?"

"Okay Majik whatever, I'm on my way" I had a full-blown attitude at this point and was seconds from hanging up on him.

"Aye, I wish yo ass would hang up on me." He knew me all too well.

"What Majik?"

"You gonna do that thing you did wit the back of your throat and yo jaws tonight?"

"Bye Majik."

"So, is that a yes or a no?" I ignored his question, he wanted to play, and I was serious "Nautica, I ain't gonna let shit happen to you girl, chill out for real. I'm always watching even when you think I'm not."

"Alright, Maj."

Only thing I could do at this point was take his word for it, I left from the school looking over my shoulder. I cleared that shit from my mind before I reached Majesti, that lil' girl was nosey as hell and would know if something was wrong with me.

By the time I made it to Majik's house I was in a better mood and was no longer thinking about the events that happened earlier. Seeing Majesti always put me in a good mood. A lot of people misunderstood her. She really was a good kid, she was just looking for someone to pay her some attention. I couldn't deny the fact that Majik loved his daughter, but let's face it, he was always ripping and running the streets, and her ratchet ass mama didn't give a shit about spending time with her. All she was worried about was spending money and shaking her ass in the club for the highest bidder.

I had been sitting in the den area with Majik for a while watching TV waiting for honey bun to wake up when I heard her running full speed down the steps, this damn girl woke up on go.

"Nauttiiiii!" she ran and jumped in my lap.

"Majiiiiiii!" I screamed back at her while tickling her.

"Oh, my goodness what took you so long? I nearly died waiting so long."

"Girl what are they teaching you at that school? You are too grown, but what's up buttercup?"

"It's time to get our day started, come on I laid out our clothes" she was talking and pulling me towards her room at the same time. We already had on clothes, so I had no idea what this girl was talking about.

Once we reached her room and I saw the matching outfits I bought us last week and it warmed my heart. I had forgotten I even bought them. After showing her, I remembered I put them in Majik's closet. I told her we could wear them another day since we were already dressed but she insisted that we put them on and what my honey bun wanted she got.

After getting on our new set of clothes which consisted of a pair of distressed jeans, a white and burgundy Gucci top, and burgundy Jordan 12s, we were on our way.

Even though we were starting our day at the nail salon, Majik insisted on driving us. That was cool with me cause I didn't wanna do all that driving today anyway. By the time we played the third Beyoncé song Majik was regretting his choice. We had our own lil' concert going on. If she wasn't so young, I'd probably buy her, and I tickets to her concert.

Walking into the nail shop I was glad it wasn't as busy as I thought it would be, it looks like we would have a wait, but not too long. I had Majesti pick out the color she wanted when it was our turn, and just as we sat down, I be damned if the devil herself didn't walk through the door. I already knew she was bout to be on some stupid shit, so I prepared myself.

We weren't even in here thirty minutes yet. Before she said anything to me, I heard her on the phone arguing with Majik about him letting her be with me. They were going back and forth, and it was a shame she was being so loud and ghetto in here. I saw her coming towards me and got myself ready for the showdown.

"Why do you keep trying play house with my kid?"

"Would you like to join us CoCo?" I decided to kill her with kindness

"Bitch do it look like I wanna join you!" Ohhh this bitch is shaking the table, in the words of K. Michelle.

She was getting a little too loud for me, and I went to stand up.

"No fight in shop," the nail tech quickly said.

Majesti put her little hand on my arm to stop me, she looked up at me scared. I took a minute and calmed down.

"CoCo I done told you about that word bitch, watch yo mouth. Now you walked your ass in this place and didn't say a damn thing to your child, yet you in here running your mouth about said, child. Girl bye!"

I was already over this conversation, so I turned around and pretended like she wasn't standing there. It's a damn shame that after I brought it to attention that she hadn't said anything to her child, she still hasn't said two words to her daughter. These men need to stop fucking everything that just looks good. Then end up with no good baby mamas.

"Damn you gonna just let her ignore you like that," ugly ass, no knowing how to fight Kaycie said.

"If you don't shut yo Helga from Hey Arnold looking ass up. I hope you here to get them eyebrows done, if not you focused on the wrong thing, sweetie."

"Ah hell naw, I know you don't have my daughter dressed like you. You can't convince me you not tryna be her mama."

"It's not that deep sweetie." I said and left it at that.

"Hey Majesti, you ready to come home yet?"

"Nah I'm good," she said not even looking up from her nails. The shit was hella funny, but she knows I didn't play about disrespect. So even though I wanted to sit there and laugh my ass off, I couldn't just sit there and not address it.

"Majesti" I gave her a look, and that's all it took. I was never mean to her, and sometimes I felt as though I was stepping outta my lane, but fuck it. She is gonna learn to be respectful.

"I'm sorry," she said to the both of us. "No, I'm not ready to come home yet, I want to stay with daddy and Nautica."

"Well yo, daddy supposed to be spending time with you, not giving you to somebody else." Look at the pot calling the fucking kettle black. This bitch got some fucking nerves.

Before I could respond to her, Majik came walking in the door with the look of murder on his face. Lord, I just want to have a peaceful rest of my day without the extra.

"Y'all bout done?" We hadn't even gotten our pedicures yet, so I told him about another hour and a half. "Aye Co, come here let me holla at you."

She knew she done fucked up by the look in her eyes, but of course in CoCo fashion she had to try to put on a show.

"Sure baby daddy anything you want" she twisted her Lil ass out the shop like she was on a runway with a smile on her face.

She may want to wipe that smile off her face cause the shit ain't gonna end well for her. Not paying any more attention to the foolishness, we finished with our nail date. He spent about five minutes outside and came back in, but CoCo wasn't with him. He shooed Helga, I mean Kaycie out and sat down with his phone in his hand.

After getting our pedicures, we were finally done, so I paid and was glad to be walking out. Getting in the car, we headed to our last stop for the night which was Chuckie Cheese. I wasn't looking forward to being around a bunch of bad ass kids running all over me, but I'd do anything for her.

MAJIK

J was sick of my dumb ass baby mama and the bullshit she was on. I was just about ready to send her to meet her cousin Tori. I didn't wanna have to do that, but the bitch was pissing me off. I hadn't even heard from her since the day she tried to act stupid in the nail shop with Nautica. Deadbeat ass ain't even checked on my daughter.

I had other shit going on at the moment, so I really didn't have time to focus on that bullshit. I finally got some info on the Baressi brothers and the shit I found out had me confused like a muthafucka. Come to find out, Solomon Baressi was Amaris and Ahnais' father. Why they were after us was baffling to me. I planned on going to holla at Ma Frankie to get some answers. We had just got a shipment in from our connect down Mexico and had to get this shit where it needed to be.

"Bruh got damn detectives came knocking on my damn door

asking bout Tori. Muthafucka said her mama crackhead ass reported her missing." Lenyx was sweating like hell as if we don't always do this on shipment day.

"Ima holla at Sampson and see what they got. They damn sho ain't got a body, so now they searching and fishing. CoCo tried coming at me wit the shit the other day."

"I shouldn't stayed with Amaris' ass when I had the chance" he was still salty now that she was all in love with that nigga Jaysun.

"Got damn man, are you bout to cry and play witcha pussy or help get this bullshit sorted?" Draiven was mad as hell.

Them fools started arguing, throwing shots at one another like a bunch of bitches. On top of that, Nautica was still being stalked by her pussy ass ex fuck boy. We took a lil trip to Chicago, but dude crib looked and smelled like he ain't been there in months. He gonna slip up though and imma be right there waiting when he does. I always got somebody watching my girl, so I ain't worried about a muthafucka touching her, it's the principle.

"Y'all gonna spend the whole time arguing like you wear thongs? We need to get a handle on these Italians."

"I got Kwame' digging a lil' deeper."

"Yeah, we need to see what he can find out. But I had Tweak from out there in Stone Mountain look into they ass too, and yeen even gonna believe this shit."

"Bitch you want a lollipop, spit the shit out," Lenyx said getting pissed.

"The Solomon cat is yo father in law," I said looking at Draiven

"Yo, what the fuck!"

"Same thing I said. I'm bout to go holla at Ma Frankie and see what she can tell me. Y'all rolling or what?"

I knew they were gonna be down to roll. They was just as eager to get to the bottom of this bullshit as I was.

We all jumped in my new 2018 Land Rover and headed to see what the hell we could find out. We've always tried to keep shit low-key as possible, so it was fucking with me they came out of nowhere on bullshit. Just as we pulled up and got out, we heard gunshots come out of nowhere. Grabbing my Glock, I ducked down quick. Frankie didn't stay in the best neighborhood, but shit rarely went on over here. This was making me believe that this wasn't random. Just as quick as it started it stopped, and I stood up and looked around to see if I could at least catch a glance the car I heard speeding away.

"Ahhh fuckkk," Draiven stood holding his shoulder, and I got even more pissed off. This shit was starting to piss me off.

I guess Frankie's nosey ass was looking out tryna see what was going on cause she came leaning out the door rushing us in.

"Who the hell y'all got over here tryna take ya out," she asked looking over at Draiven bleeding.

"We'll get to that in a minute. Can you do something bout this shit though?" This nigga was crying like a whole bitch out here.

"Boy shut the hell up, it's just a flesh wound and you crying. If you cry what Yanni gone do?"

After she said that I had to get up and look for myself and I be damn his ass was just grazed. This grown ass man over there whining like he done been shot five times. She stitched him up, and it was time to get down to why we were here.

"Frankie we need to holla at you bout some shit."

"That's why y'all came over here like the Men in Black?" I wanted to laugh, but this was important, and I didn't have time for it.

"Ma stop playing this shit seriously, life or death, hell maybe yours too. Who is Solomon Barassi?"

By the look on her face, she knew exactly who it was and was scared shitless. That reaction alone had me on high alert. I've never seen her look so serious about anything.

"Wha wha why umm why are you asking about him?"

"Some shit been going down and that name been thrown around. Solomon and Roman, so what can you tell me about them?"

She was clearly thinking bout what she wanted to say. I didn't need to be bullshitted right now, I didn't have time for it.

Solomon is the father of my kids. I met him when I was a freshman in high school. He was four years older and was always in the streets, his father was a big deal in Atlanta. When he got me pregnant the first time I was paid to stay away, but Solomon refused, I thought after he did that we'd be together forever. Ha joke was on me" she had tears rolling down her face as she relived her pain of her past "right after Ahnais was born, I had another visit from his father, but this time he had a woman with him. Long story short she was Solomon's wife, he had no intention of marrying me. Once he left he never looked back, not even one birthday card. Oh but I did get word from the Barassi's, if I contacted Solomon or told anybody that he was their father, they would kill me. I haven't heard from that bastard since."

This shit was bugging me the fuck out. What the hell they Jerry Springer, Maury shit gotta do with me?

"Okay y'all got baby mama, baby daddy issues, so what the fuck we gotta do with that?"

"I don't know what's going on or why he would have issues with y'all."

I was just as confused as I was when I got here. Nothing she told us gave me any insight on what them pasta eating, pink toe muthafuckas wanted with us. I was due to meet up with Marcelo our connect next week, so I was gonna run this by him. He was like family, so I always trusted his judgment.

Two weeks later...

Me, Draiven, and Lenyx had just touched down in Mexico, and it was muggy as hell out here. I ain't want shit now but a shower. I sent Nautica a message checking on her and Majesti before I did anything else. Marcelo had a car waiting for us, so we headed to his compound. Now that is some shit I can't wait to have. His estate was big enough to build four or five huge mansions.

As soon as we pulled up, we were bombarded with workers , some grabbing our bags, showing us in and moving, and just doing the most. That's one thing I could do without, I don't like a lot of folks around me. I need to be able to keep my eyes on everybody.

"Hola mis hijos, Que bueno verte'" Marcelo's wife Carmen greeted us. She always showed us nothing but great hospitality when we came to her home.

"Hola señora Carmen. Cómo estás?" We each respectfully placed a kiss on her cheek as we were lead to her husband's study.

Normally I'd go get settled first in the room that was available for me when I came but being that we were only staying until first thing in the morning, I didn't bother bringing much. All I had with me was an overnight bag, which was enough for me in my opinion. With Nautica's ex still fucking with her and these Italians causing unknown problems, there was no way I was gonna leave my family without me there with them for too long.

"Mi Familia, hola. How are things going?" Marcelo asked in his thick Spanish accent.

"You know how we do, money looking real good," Lenyx said rubbing his hands together like he was Birdman.

For the next hour or so we sat back discussing future shipments. I thought it was best that we change shit around considering all the shit that was going on. One could never ever be too careful when it comes to money.

"Now that that's out ti way, I have shumting I need to speak to you boys about."

"Not to cut you off Celo, but we got something to run by you first," Draiven scooted up to the edge of his seat as he started talking. "We been having a lil issue round the way with some cats that damn near came outta nowhere. We had a few people check it out and found out it's some fuck ass Italians. The name Barassi came about, but the sick shit is it's supposedly my girl's pops. Now we ain't asking for you to handle shit for us, but you think you can get your people to dig a little deeper."

"Did you say Barassi?"

The crinkle in his forehead paired with the thick accented anger in voice had me sitting straight up

"Yeah, a Solomon and Roman Barassi. You know em?" We all were eagerly waiting.

"HIJO DE PUTA" whoever these Barassi's are, they sho is ruffling some feathers "that is why I needed to see you guys. I'm getting too old for this shit, it's time for me to relax and enjoy life with Carmen. I'm looking for someone I can pass this on to and that someone is you three."

Me, Lenyx, and Draiven all looked at each other in surprise "that got damn Solomon been a pain in my ass for years. He wants my fields. He knows I'm getting out and probably handing someone my spot, which comes with my fields. He's coming for you that means he's coming for me." He finished with a look of irritation.

We had a lot to think about. I left Mexico with more on my mind than I came with. At least we had a little more information on these Italians and wasn't walking around here blind. I hurried and carried my ass home, I was in need of a nice fat blunt and some pussy.

LENYX

*I*f it ain't one thing, it's a got damn nother. CoCo and her bum ass family keep coming to me about Tori. I have an alibi, a strong one at that, so I ain't even worried bout it. We got the chief of police on our payroll anyway, so this shit ain't going nowhere. Shit shouldn't have never slipped past him. He'll have to see me bout that.

I'd been out since seven this morning collecting money from our trap houses. We damn near controlled the Westside of Atlanta. After being out all day with crazy ass Turk my ass was finally done. I never worried bout handling shit with Turk cause this fool was one of the most thoroughbred ass niggas I've come across in a long time. I made sure he was promoted up every chance there was.

I was headed to one of the new warehouses that we had

gotten right before our Mexico trip. I took so many turns and side streets I damn near got confused myself.

I was finally done handling business, so I was now time to see what was up for the day. I had plans later to check out this chick I'd met at the club last week. She'd been blowing my shit up since the day I met her ass.

Pulling into the gas station, I grabbed my ringing phone, and I pulled into an open spot. Looking to the left of me I saw a fine ass chick I just had to holla at.

"What up fool?" I answered still keeping my eyes on shawty.

"The hell yo Sideshow Bob looking ass doing?" Draiven always calling fucking with folks.

"What you want fuck boy?" This nigga needed to hurry up before Ms. Fine ass got away. I hated talking on the phone next to the gas pumps and couldn't stand to see other muthafuckas doing it. That was the most unsafe thing you could do.

"We throwing some shit on the grill since the weather nice out, bring ya ugly ass over. We done already got started."

"Aight, I'm on the way. Tell my baby Ahnais to keep it warm for me, daddy coming."

"Don't make me kill you, Len." He said serious as fuck and hung up on me.

I laughed cause I knew he was mad as shit. He didn't play 'bout his light, bright girl. That's my brother so of course, I'd never go there, but it was always good to mess with him.

I made it in the store to pay for my gas just as shawty walked up to the register. Seeing her up close, she was even more beautiful than I thought she was.

"How you doing Ms. Lady?" she turned around with the look of annoyance, "damn shawty it's like that?"

"Look I'm not interested. Have a nice day."

"Maybe if you fixed your fucking attitude you'd be having a better day."

I walked up to the next register and handed them the money for my purchase and gas and walked out. I wasn't in the business of chasing no bitch. I was just about done pumping my gas when she walked out the store and looked my way. Her face softened up kinda, but I wasn't bout to try and get at her again. Fuck that bitch!

When I pulled up to the Draiven and Ahnais' house, it looked like everybody was here and partying it up. They lucky it was my day to collect or I'd be pissed. It was muthafuckas here that I ain't never seen before, so off top, I was scoping out the scene. I always had my guard up no matter what.

I made it over to where Draiven was burning shit up on the grill. Nigga swore up and down he was the grill master and wasn't shit but the master burner. I spoke to everyone and grabbed me a beer out the cooler.

"Hey, brother, what took you so long?" Amaris and Ahnais both came over to speak.

"Shit what you mean, this egg head ass nigga just called me bout an hour or so ago and told me about it."

"You an ole snitchin' ass muthafucka."

Ahnais gave him the death stare, and it was funny to see how scared he was. He probably was supposed to been had let me know.

"Cut em some slack sis, I know you missed me and shit, but I'm here now." I gave her a hug just to be extra to get up under his skin.

"Keep on fucking with me and watch you leave here with a bullet in ya ass."

Everybody around laughed and continued enjoying themselves. Right after my nieces Yanni and Majesti came over draining my pockets I quickly fixed me a plate and sat right back down. I must've been hungry cause I was going in on that food and wasn't paying attention to a damn thing going on around me, especially not when Ahnais walked back over.

"Hey, brother let me introduce you to somebody," if she knew how hungry I was she'd save this shit for another time. Wiping my mouth I finally looked up and got pissed just that quick "this is Selina, she's one of the pharmacy technicians down at my job. Selina this is my brother Lenyx."

There in front of me stood the cutie from the gas station. She looked to be in a better mood, but I wasn't fucking wit it.

"We sorta met already," she told Ahnais, "hello Lenyx."

"Sup" I was being petty and giving her the same attitude she had given me.

Sis smiled and walked away, saying she 'd give us a moment alone. I don't know why, hell, I'm good on shawty.

Majik walked over and said he needed to holla at me a Draiven and when I started to get up ole girl stopped me.

"Can I talk to you for a second please?"

I stood there with my arms folded over my chest and waited for her to say whatever it was she needed to say.

"I just wanted to tell you I was sorry for being a bitch back at the store. I'd had a really bad day, but it was no reason to take it out on you. Can we start over please?"

Not saying a word I continued to just stand there looking at her for a few seconds. I guess everyone was entitled to a bad day every now and again, so I'll let shawty have that this one time.

"Yeah I guess, but for the future, you shouldn't go around taking your bad day out on people. You never know who you may be missing out on meeting. I woulda hated for you to have had to miss out on a nigga like me."

When she smiled it just added to her beauty. I forgot all about Majik needing to chop it up with us. Once I started talking to Selina, we kinda fell into a good ass conversation. I learned a lot about her, and she was a pretty dope chic. We all know how that goes though. Females had a way of making themselves seem better than what they really were. I'mma see what shawty was about though.

AMARIS

S ome crazy shit been going on lately. I guess that ain't nothing new for our family though, we always got some bullshit going on. Everywhere I go, I have been seeing the same man. He looks like he could be Hispanic or an Italian. Whatever he is, the shit was freaking me out. I was gonna have to make sure I let Jaysun and my brothers know. Somebody could be out here plotting to get my good old goodies. Maybe if I was to eat a big bag of Funyuns, walk up to buddy, ask him if he wanna smell my punanie, and blow in his face like ole girl on Poetic Justice, he might just run away like Tupac did.

A nigga gonna have to work hard if he thinks he gonna grab me up and take my snatch. I'm pissing, farting, and shitting all on that nigga. He gonna think twice before try doing it again to somebody else.

I was at the grocery store grabbing up some stuff to make Jaysun's favorite meal, Chicken and Shrimp Alfredo. I never used that jar sauce, so everything was made from scratch. I didn't mind though, I was willing to do anything that would make him feel better. He'd been really missing Destiny this week and feeling down. I think about her every day and wish like hell I'd had more time with her. Throwing himself deeper into the streets is what he called coping; I don't say shit I just let him be.

At the checkout counter, I saw that same man, and it irritated me. I went ahead and sent a text out to both Jaysun and Majik.

Jaysun: why some Hispanic or Italian man been following me around. Been seeing him every damn where I go lately. Niggas ain't getting my goodies

Majik: why some Hispanic or Italian man been following me around. Been seeing him every damn where I go lately. Niggas ain't getting my goodies

Once I left the store I headed to go see my crazy ass mama, I hadn't seen her all week. Just as I pulled into the driveway, I was getting a call from Majik.

"Whashhh poppin' tho?"

"Where you at sis? Need to holla at you bout something."

"Is it 'bout whoever following me? I'm just pulling up to mama's house though." He sounded too serious.

"I'm on the way through there big head ass girl."

"Ya daughter the one wit a big ass head and ya girlfriend. Bye nigga!" I hung up before he had a chance to have a comeback.

Before I was able to put my phone up and get out the car my damn phone started ringing again and this time it was Jaysun.

"Hey, babe!"

"Hey, baby, where you at?" I feel like this is *Where in the world is Carmen Sandiego.*

"I just got to mama house. Let me guess you on the way?"

"Yeah, I'll be there in a minute. Oh and do me a favor, keep ya smart as remarks to a minimum.

"Love youuuu, mean ittttt."

Finally able to get out and make my way inside my mama's house, I was hoping she had something sweet for me to eat. I had a sweet tooth like a muthafucka. My mama was a beast at baking, and I was craving her sweet treats.

I used my key to open the door, but I was a little hesitant about not knocking first. She was always talking about she got shit to do, who knows what that shit is. She could be acting like Stella, and tryna get her old ass groove back. You never know with Frankie.

I went walking through the house to find her, and I found her in the living room watching episodes of *Love and Hip Hop Atlanta.* Why in the hell couldn't she be watching something like reruns of *The Andy Griffin show* or *Judge Mathis?* She's so damn old and ghetto.

"Heyyy old lady, what you doing up in here?"

"The hell it looks like and why you just walking yo lil ass up in my house?"

I don't know why she always tryna play hard. She knows she be missing us just was much as we miss her.

"Mama why you gotta act like that? I was missing you and wanted to come see you."

"Child stop all that damn whining! What's been going on with you."

These are the moments that I cherished and loved to have. My mama wasn't getting any younger, so I was happy to spend this time with her. Even if she was cursing me out in the meantime. We were talking for quite a while about everything under the sun. Just as we were getting deep into our conversation, there was a knock on the door. I figured it was one of the guys, but when I went to open the door, it was both of them. I was about to joke with them, but the look on their faces made me change my mind. They told me to step outside so now I was really concerned.

"Mama I'mma go on the porch to holla at Jaysun and Majik."

They both spoke, and we stepped outside. I don't know if I was prepared for whatever they were about to tell me.

"I'mma make this short and sweet, I was on my way to give your cousin some of this mid-day dick."

"TMI," I interrupted him."

"Anyway, it's some shit going on, we don't have everything single detail on it, but I did fill yo man in so he won't be out here in the blind. I need you to keep your eyes and ears open at all times. For now on, you and Ahnias will have someone following y'all. We shoulda been doing it, that's our fuck up."

"Are we in danger?" I was no longer joking and shaking like hell I was so scared, I hated the unknown.

I don't know what the hell going on but I wanted my mama with me just in case. I know when muthafuckas got beef they always went for family members. I'll go up against the Russian Mob by myself bout my Lady.

"Y'all straight sis" was all he said.

"Babe chill out man, I ain't gone let shit happen to ya ass. Not unless you try to hold out on that pussy and then I'm handing you right the fuck over." He laughed and ran into the house as I went to take off his dome.

"You got Nauti right? She already got to worry about that punk ass ex of hers."

"You already know sis that goes without saying. I can't wait to put a bullet in his ass."

"Good, she done been through too much. She don't need any more bullshit coming her way."

"You already know I got her. I can't wait to put a bullet in his ass."

I was still outside talking to Majik's looney ass when two groups of young girls started arguing out of nowhere. I bet money they were arguing over a nigga. I wish I could school these youngins, but it wasn't gonna be today cause I was too into this fight they just started. These lil ratchet ass heffas was out there putting on a show, shit was going better than one of Floyd Mayweather fights. We were cracking up and having our own commentary. Nautica's ass called just as someone ran over to break them up. Her horny ass was rushing bro home, so he went to holla at mama before he left.

I stood on the porch in a daze just thinking. I don't know what is going on, but I know this comes with the territory. Dating someone in this lifestyle, you never know what will come your way. I don't want to ever have to bury Jaysun or one of my brothers. I love all their asses.

MAMA FRANKIE

2 *0 years ago…*
   I been waiting all day for Solomon to make it over to
the house. He'd promised to take me and the girls out, and I was
excited. I'd love Solomon Barassi since I was fourteen years old.
I dressed the girls in matching pink and white dresses with the
cutest little pink sandals and let their hair out in its naturally
curly state.

   Hearing a car door close I got up and checked myself in the
mirror while anticipating a knock on the door. As soon as I heard
that first knock, my heart starts beating with nervousness as I
always get nervous around him. I opened the door with a smile,
but it immediately fades once I saw it wasn't Solomon on the
other side. There stood a much taller version of him and a
woman I, of course, didn't know.

   "Yes, may I help you?" I asked.

"Hello, you may not know who I am, my name is Gennaro. May I come in please?" I'm now nervous thinking I was about to receive some bad news about Solomon and already was ready to shed tears as I led them in my home.

"What is this about?"

"I understand you have dealings with my son Solomon," his Italian accent was thicker than some of these bitches edges "I'm here to let you know that is no more. You will no longer deal with him. This is Viviana, she is the woman he is set to marry."

I looked at her as she looked back at me with a smirk. I still didn't believe all of this was real. There is no way Solomon would lead me on, our love is real.

"I'm sorry, I'm going to need Solomon to tell me this, I don't believe you."

"Look you will stay away from my son. There is no room for you and those nigger babies in my world. If you want those babies of yours to stay alive, you will do as you are told and stay away from my son. Here is a little something for your troubles," he said throwing an envelope on the nearby table and turning to walk out the door. "If I hear you did not adhere to my wishes it will not end well for you my dear." And just like that, he was gone.

I waited to hear from Solomon for two weeks until I realized he had played me. He was a coward and had left his kids behind.

I never knew the shit from my past would come to bite me in the ass like this. I have no idea what Solomon's pasta eating ass is up to, but I know it ain't good. He was just as evil as his bitch ass daddy. I wish I wouldn't have never fucked around with his ass. The only good thing about him was his dick. I did everything I could to stay out their path. Now here I am having to temporarily move into my daughter's home. I fought tooth and nails, but my son in law wasn't having it. I was supposed to move with Amaris, but Draiven insisted I come with them. I know it's just so I could deal with Yanni's ass. One thing I know is I couldn't wait until all this was over. I was ready to get my life back.

DRAIVEN

$\mathcal{I}$ felt like I was about to lose my mind. I'd been running around for days tryna get shit together for this dinner I had planned for Ahnais. She been having an attitude since yesterday, of course, she thinks I'm up to no good. I had one thing I left I needed to handle before the dinner tomorrow, and that was handle this Tatiana situation.

I was on the way to meet Majik and Lenyx so I could finally get this shit over with. This bitch has been a pain in my ass ever since she drugged me. Calling my phone threatening me, tryna expose me until she found out my girl already knew. I just been going along with the shit. I pulled up to Lenyx house with my all black on ready for war. Knowing I was bout to end this bitch was enough to make my dick hard. I walked in his shit like I owned it, I was just waiting for him to say something smart.

"Nigga don't be walking yo Ron Stoppable looking ass in my

shit like you pay bills," he said walking into the living room with the phone glued to his ear.

Ever since we had the lil barbecue at my house a few weeks ago, his ass ain't been doing shit but up Selina ass. I hope he checked her out cause I won't mind putting a bullet in her head if she on some fuck shit.

"I'll burn this shit down with yo Casper the friendly ghostly looking ass in it," he swung tryna hit me, and I ducked. "Aight keep on with yo light, bright ass and I'ma clap you the fuck off."

I had Majik dying laughing, and Len could say shit, he just shot me a bird and went back to caking. I got in a game of NBA2K18 wit Majik until it was time to go handle business.

It was finally 1 a.m., and we loaded up in the chop shop car we got so it couldn't be traced. Shit was gonna be ashes after this was over with anyway. We came up on Tatiana's house and scoped the scene. Them muthafuckas had her living it up. I cut the electricity off, and Lenyx was able to pick through the lock. It was dark as hell, but with the night goggles we copped, we were able to see everything.

Going from room to room we finally came up on the one she was in. This bitch was knocked out all peacefully like her life wasn't in danger. I had Len cut the lights back on cause I needed this bitch to see my face before we killed her ass.

"Wakey wakey lil bitty bitch" tapping her forehead with my pistol, I woke her up out her sleep.

She jumped up looking around. When her eyes focused and landed on me, fear took over, and she went to try to scream.

"Scream and I'mma make sure to kill you nice and slow."

"Wait Draiven, you don't have to do this. I'm sorry, I promise I'll leave you alone."

"What happened to that tough girl shit?"

She sat there crying like that shit was supposed to move me. I didn't give a damn bout them tears.

"Tell me what you know about them muthafuckas you work for?" Majik said

"I-I um I don't know what you're talking about."

Before she got the words out, Majik shot her in the arm "Ahhhhh! OK OK!"

"Stop fucking playing with me bitch. I can do this shit all night."

"There isn't much I can tell you, I've been working for them for years and was told to get close to y'all. I was told to disrupt your home and throw you off your square. I don't know what they have planned for y'all but they coming hard."

This bitch wasn't telling me shit, and I was tired of playing with her.

"How many times did you text me trying to blackmail me?" She shrugged her shoulders looking stupid "look at your phone and see."

She grabbed her phone, and I stood next to her to make sure she wasn't tryna no funny shit.

"Twelve, it was twelve times."

"Alright then," I said as I shot her in the other arm.

I ignored her screams as I continued to shoot her in different parts of her body. I made sure to shoot her in places that would kill her slowly. She was still alive, barely hanging on. For the final twelfth shot, I hit her with a headshot that damn near took her head off. Turning on her stove and the gas, we got the fuck up out of there, and before we turned the corner, her shit exploded. It was no way that body would be found. Once we made it back to Lenyx's house, I jumped in my car and took my ass home. I was relieved that shit was finally over.

I woke up the next day nervous as hell. Tonight was the night, and I needed everything to go off as planned. I called the restaurant twice to make sure everything was set up the way I asked. Ahnais had to go into work for a few hours today, so I sent her a text letting her know we had dinner with the family tonight. Of course, she thought it celebrating one of our problems being handled. After I got the confirmation that everything was in order, I chilled around the house for the remainder of the day.

*L*ater that night…
        I jumped in the shower and handled my hygiene, I'd been laying around all day, so I know my nuts was funky. I planned on being knee deep in my girl's guts tonight, so I needed to be good and fresh. It didn't take me long to wash my ass, lotion up, and throw on my clothes I had hanging up in the closet. I had bought all of us some shit to wear tonight, we was bout to be on our fly shit.

Of course, Ahnais was taking all got damn day to get ready. We were gonna be late for our own damn dinner reservation if she didn't hurry up.

"Ahnais, what the hell is taking you so long? You've had plenty of time to get ready man"!

"Chill out damn, I'm almost ready. I just gotta change purses."

Twenty minutes later we were finally walking out the door. It didn't take long for us to make it to the restaurant, so we were pulling up in no time. I was breaking all kind of laws getting us there. I'm glad Mama Frankie had rode with Amaris, or she'd be cussing my ass the fuck out.

I let the hostess know we had a reservation and she led us to the private room they'd set up. Everyone was already here, and I was glad. I wanted to get this shit over with as quick as possible. My damn stomach was doing all kind of flips, and I was farting like a muthafucka.

"Auntie you look so pretty" Majesti came up to her and said.

"Thank you, baby, so do you." She kissed her on the cheek, and she ran back to her seat.

"Sis I know you glad that bitch is out the way," Amaris said taking a sip of her drink.

"Girl I was bout ready to get at that bitch myself."

"I know how you feel cause I'm bout ready to take me out a bitch" Nautica spoke up giving Majik a mean ass mug.

"Don't start that shit man."

Ain't no telling what that shit was about. CoCo known for doing stupid ass shit, so it wasn't no telling.

We had gotten through our meal, and it was that time. I was sweating like a hoe in church. I gave the waitress the signal to let her know it was that time.

The music started playing, and I had my homeboy Shawn come out singing. That was a true gangsta through and through, but he could sing his ass off.

I found love in you

And I've learned to love me too

Never have I felt that I could be all that you see

It's like our hearts have intertwined and to the perfect harmony

I stood up just when the song was coming to an end as Ahnais looked around trying to figure out what was going on. Getting on my knee, I began to speak from my heart.

"Oh my God Oh my God oh my God!" She said knowingly bouncing up and down.

"I told you when we first met that I would one day make you my wife. You have made me a better man, and I can't imagine living life without you. Every day I imagine what it will be like to grow old with you and raise a shitload of kids that look just like you. You are the most beautiful woman I've ever seen. I want to spend the rest of my life loving you, providing for you, and being the man you want me to be. Ahnais Janae Davenport will you marry me?"

Pulling the ring box from my pocket, I opened it as I looked up at her and wiped the tears that were falling from her eyes.

"Yes, yes, yes!"

Standing up and hugged her lifting her off her feet. I wasn't done yet though. I had one more thing I needed to do. Walking over to my baby girl Yanni, I got back on my knee and grabbed her hand.

"What are you doing daddy?"

"The first day you called me daddy was one of the best days of my life. I'd never imagined having a daughter as beautiful as you. I want to spend the rest of my life loving you, teaching you, guiding you, and showing you how a man is supposed to treat you. If you will have me, I want to officially be your daddy and give you my last name... what you say kiddo, can I be your daddy?"

"That means I'll have you and mommy's name?"

"That's right baby girl."

She leaped into my arms and wrapped her arms around my neck as tight as she could. I kissed the side of her head and hugged her back.

"I love you, daddy."

"Love you more Yanni."

I handed her mother the adoption papers that I had gotten. I'd already filled out my part, I just needed her to fill out hers.

Everyone stood up congratulating us, and the girls, of course, were giving me their don't fuck up speeches. We were standing around chopping it up in our own world when we were interrupted by the sounds of someone clapping.

Clap clap clap clap

"That was a beautiful proposal, my nigga, I hope y'all can come to me and my girl's wedding soon. Ain't that right Nautica?"

I don't know who the fuck this nigga was, but he was bout to get his ass killed.

"Yo who the fuck is this bitch ass muthafucka?" Majik asked Nautica pulling out his Glock.

"Draego," she whispered and moved behind him scared.

Shit, he pulled out his strap and me and Lenyx did the same. I felt Ahnais shaking, and I turn to look at her, and she was crying with nothing but fear in her eyes.

"Babe, why are you shaking, what's the matter?"

"That's him, that's him, that's the man that raped me!" She said and fainted.

What the fuck!

To be continued....

Join my reading group and social media pages to stay up to date with future releases and sneak peeks.

Facebook: D.Nika's Reading Divas
Author Page: Author D.Nika
Instagram: Nicamonique31

CPSIA information can be obtained
at www.ICGtesting.com
Printed in the USA
LVHW091620220219
608477LV00002B/161/P